TO CATCH A MAN
(IN 30 DAYS OR LESS)

JUDY ANGELO

JUDY ANGELO

The BAD BOY BILLIONAIRES Series
Volume 8

BAD BOY BILLIONAIRES
Volume 1 – Tamed by the Billionaire
Volume 2 – Maid in the USA
Volume 3 - Billionaire's Island Bride
Volume 4 - Dangerous Deception
Volume 5 - To Tame a Tycoon
Volume 6 - Sweet Seduction
Volume 7 - Daddy by December
Volume 8 - To Catch a Man (in 30 Days or Less)
Volume 9 – Bedding Her Billionaire Boss
Volume 10 - Her Indecent Proposal
Volume 11 - So Much Trouble When She Walked In
Volume 12 – Married by Midnight

. . ⤬ . .

THE BILLIONAIRE BROTHERS KENT
Book 1 - The Billionaire Next Door
Book 2 - Babies for the Billionaire
Book 3 - Billionaire's Blackmail Bride
Book 4 - Bossing the Billionaire

. . ⤬ . .

COLLECTIONS
BAD BOY BILLIONAIRES, Coll. I - Vols. 1 - 4
BAD BOY BILLIONAIRES, Coll. II - Vols. 5 - 8
BAD BOY BILLIONAIRES, Coll. III - Vols. 9 - 12
THE BILLIONAIRE BROS. KENT - Books 1 - 4
BAD BOY BILLIONAIRES, Double Coll. - Vols. 1 - 8
BAD BOY BILLIONAIRES, Mega Coll. - Vols. 1 - 12

. . ✿ . .

HOLIDAY EDITIONS
Rome for the Holidays - Novella
Rome for Always - Full-length Novel

. . ✿ . .

The NAUGHTY AND NICE Series
Volume 1 - Naughty by Nature

. . ✿ . .

COMING SOON
THE CASTILLOS
Book 1 - Beauty and the Beastly Billionaire

. . ✿ . .

judyangeloauthor@gmail.com

TO CATCH A MAN (IN 30 DAYS OR LESS)

. . ❧ . .

HOW DO YOU CATCH A MAN...IN 30 DAYS?

Indiana Lane is in a pickle. She must find a man, fall in love and get married...all within the space of thirty days. How in the world can she pull this off? And then she runs into Stone Hudson - or, more accurately, he runs into her - and that's when the adventure begins.

Stone Hudson has met his match. He is used to women fawning over him and then he meets Indie, a woman who tells it like it is. And worse, she dares to tease him wherever and whenever she desires. Stone is intrigued, to say the least, but then his heart is snagged on a wire from which there is no escape.

Will the wedding bells ring for Indie, and will they ring in time? Thirty days is not a lot of time...

CHAPTER ONE

"Are you kidding me?"

Randolph Marshall shook his head. "I'm dead serious. You have until October twenty-three or you forfeit fourteen million dollars."

"Fourteen million..." Indiana Lane's voice trailed off as she stared across the desk at the attorney. "No, you've got to be kidding me." She looked around the room. "I'm on 'Candid Camera', right? Or one of those other crazy prank shows?" She began to chuckle as she turned to look back at him.

"Miss Lane, trust me. I do not have time for pranks." Exasperation dripped from each word. "I'm an old man with a bad heart. I don't play games. I tell it as it is. Do you understand me?"

Indie's smile began to fade as she stared back at the now frowning man. Okay, so he really was serious. He was shaking his graying head and looking at her like he wanted to give her a sharp rap on the knuckles. Ouch.

"Yes," she said, gripping the arms of the chair, "I understand you but...but he hardly even knew me."

Marshall looked unimpressed. "He seems to have known you well enough to want to make you a rich woman. Under certain conditions, of course."

"But...but..." She was spluttering again. *Come on, Indie, this is so not like you. You've negotiated with guerilla fighters and warlords and you're thrown upside down by this?* She drew in a slow, deep breath then got up and shoved her hands deep into her trouser pockets. Her brain worked better when she was standing.

"So let me get this straight. Based on the stipulations in my uncle's will I have to find a man in the next..." she frowned, thinking, "...thirty days, fall in love, and get married in order to inherit this fourteen million dollars?"

Randolph cocked a grizzly eyebrow. "Nobody said anything about falling in love."

"Well, I can't very well just run off and marry the next man I run into, can I? One would hope I'd at least feel something for him...and he, for me." She stopped talking when she saw the attorney's expression. Was the man laughing at her?

"A real idealist, I see." His smile was broader than the Cheshire Cat's.

That got her riled up. "And who says I want his money, anyway?" The man was looking too smug and it was pissing her off. Big time. "Money has never been the biggest thing in my life, Mr. Randolph Marshall. And neither has marriage. I can do without both of them-"

"Yes, Miss 'Save-The-World'. I know. And that's exactly why your uncle did what he did. Don't you worry. He filled me in on all the details."

Now on top of pissing her off he was confusing the heck out of her. "What details?"

"Remember that conversation you had with him right after your mother's funeral?"

She frowned. "That was nine years ago."

"Yes," Randolph said with a nod. "You were twenty-one years old and you sat in the library spouting off your idealistic philosophies to Samuel about not wanting to get married or have children. There are too many homeless kids in the world for you to even think of starting a family of your own. Isn't that what you said?"

Indie straightened to her full five foot nine inch height and frowned at Marshall. What was he getting at? "Yeah, so what? I still think the same way."

Marshall nodded slowly. "Ah-ha. And that's what your uncle was afraid of." He leaned forward and propped his elbows on the desk. "You're going to be thirty years old in thirty days, Indiana. Thirty. Think of it. That old, and no man and no kids. No life except for running off to the favelas of Brazil to save orphans or chopping through the bushes and jungles of Colombia to search out drug dealers selling girls as sex slaves. Where were you this time? Africa?"

"Haiti," she said, her tone sullen.

The lawyer heaved a sigh. "Haiti. And where next? Cambodia?" He shook his head. "Listen. Your uncle wants his bloodline to continue. He never had kids and you, his sister's child, are his only hope of that. He wants you to get cracking while your eggs are still viable."

"He what?" Indie almost burst out laughing. The audacity of the man. "He actually said that?"

"Yes, and more, but..." Marshall put his hand up, "you don't want to know." He leaned back in his chair and clasped his hands behind his head. "So, are you on board? Can I cross you off my list of things to do this month and consider this sealed and set?"

Indie could only shake her head in disbelief. Between the lawyer and her now dead uncle she didn't know which one was battier. They'd probably both been smoking the same...prohibited substance.

"Now you listen to me, Mr. Marshall." She fixed him with a glare of defiance. "I have two things to say to you. Number one, I don't want a single dime of Uncle Sam's fourteen million dollars. I've gotten along quite well without his help and will continue to survive, I'm sure. And number two," she raised an eyebrow, "if he'd wanted me to be married, barefoot and pregnant by age thirty he should have spoken a heck of a lot earlier than September twenty-three."

For a long moment Marshall just stared at her, his lips pursed, then he nodded solemnly. "Well said, but let me implore you to think about it. You're so concerned about doing good in the world, do you know how much more you could do with fourteen million dollars?" He paused as if to let that sink in. "And as for the timing, I think I know what happened." He glanced down, shifted a couple of papers, then picked up the will. He reached for his glasses, put them on then peered at the document. "Yes," he said with a sigh, "I was right. He miscalculated your age. When he updated this four years ago he had you down as twenty-four years old but you were actually twenty-five." He looked up at her, peering over the top of his glasses like an old owl. "I guess he was planning to tell you but was biding his time, watching to see if things would work out. Probably thought he had at least a few more months before he had to tackle you on such a touchy subject." He shrugged. "Who was to know he'd have been taken out by a heart attack at age sixty-six?"

Marshall's speech had Indie staring at him in shock. She was so worked up she didn't know what to say. Then she snorted. "Yeah, right. He thought I was a year younger? Do you realize if he hadn't died when he did I would have soon passed his stupid deadline for me? I'll be thirty in a month."

"Yeah, well." Marshall shrugged. "If he'd lived he probably would have updated the will. The pity is, he never got a chance to realize or correct his miscalculation. And with him being dead, you're stuck with it."

"This is so stupid," Indie muttered as she began to pace the room. "Stupid, stupid."

"I know. But it is what it is. Fourteen million dollars or zilch. Your call." The lawyer began to slide the documents back into the case. "You know where to find me, Indiana. I leave everything in your hands. Just remember the date – October twenty-three, by midnight."

And with that, Indie knew she was being dismissed. The man had other clients to deal with, other more pressing business. He was probably checking the clock to make sure she didn't run over her portion of his 'billable hour' or whatever it was lawyers called it.

And at the same time he was dismissing her he'd thrown her normally well-ordered life into a whirlpool of indecision. Where in the world should she go from here? And if she did decide to fulfill Sam's condition where the heck should she start looking for a man to marry...in thirty days?

STONE HUDSON SKIPPED channels, trying desperately to find a station with music that would keep him awake. The evening traffic was brutal, jamming up all the way from Oakville. He wouldn't make it to Burlington for another thirty minutes at this rate. He heaved a sigh and surfed more channels.

He was one tired son-of-a-gun, up for the past twenty-two hours since leaving Johannesburg the day before. The valet had brought his car and he'd driven out of the Toronto Pearson Airport exactly thirty-eight minutes ago but still he was only a little more than halfway home.

Stubborn brute that he was, he'd insisted on driving his Maserati home. Now he could only shake his head in regret. This was one of those days when he should have let the chauffeur come and get him. Damn him for always having to be in control. He hated being in a vehicle where he wasn't the one behind the wheel but that ultra-independent trait of his was certainly working against him this evening.

He shook his head and blinked to clear the cobwebs from his eyes then stifled a yawn. He turned the radio up as loud as he could stand it and the air conditioning to full blast. It was going to be rough going, trying to stay awake in traffic that was almost at a standstill.

Maroon five's 'One More Night' was pounding in his ears when traffic got unplugged and began to move. Finally. A slight smile crept across his lips. The images were so vivid now – home, a soothing bath, bed, sliding under the cool sheets, his head sinking into the soft pillows, closing his weary eyes-

Wham!

Stone's head jerked up and he slammed on the brake. What the-

He blinked. And then he groaned. He'd run into the back of an army-green Land Rover. Christ!

Cursing himself for being such a clutz he began to pull over onto the soft shoulder. The Land Rover was pulling over, too. He groaned. Just what he needed. A rear-ending as a fitting close to his journey of almost twenty-four hours. He'd learned his lesson – no more pretending to be Superman on these long trips.

Stone grabbed his wallet off the front passenger's seat and slid out of the car. Reaching up to massage the back of his neck he stifled another yawn. God, he was tired. He blinked to clear the gravel from his eyes then walked over to meet the guy who was climbing out of the Land Rover.

A quick glance told Stone his Maserati hadn't suffered a scratch. The other vehicle was another matter. It now sported a smashed-in back bumper. He steeled himself for the swearing. This was going to be one pissed-off dude.

The other driver was coming toward him now, a slender kid of medium height with short black hair that glistened in the sun. Plaid shirt rolled up at the sleeves, jeans and Timberland boots, he must have been coming from work. *Sorry to spoil the end of your work day, kid.*

Stone glanced down and began digging his driver's license out of his wallet. When he looked up again the kid was standing right in front of him, green eyes flashing, soft pink lips set in an angry pout.

Huh? Stone's gaze dropped to the plaid-covered chest and there, pert and pointing straight at him, was his confirmation. The dude was a girl.

"Hey, what's up with you, fella? Falling asleep at the wheel?"

Stone frowned. Kind of aggressive, wasn't she? It was when she got closer that he saw that she wasn't so much a girl as she was a woman, probably in her late twenties, maybe about four or five years younger than he was. And she was tall. Well, for a woman. The top of her head was just shy of his earlobe and he was six foot three.

And her eyes, so like those of a cat, were practically cutting him to shreds. With her high cheekbones, long nose and tanned skin she looked like a Native American princess. But it was those eyes, like green shards of glass fringed with incredibly long lashes, that had him staring like a dumbstruck fool.

"What? Cat got your tongue?"

It took that sarcastic remark to snap him out of his daze. He scowled. He wasn't used to being on the receiving end of such biting remarks, least of all from a woman. Most of the women he knew would be falling over themselves to impress him. At least, the ones who knew who he was.

He didn't bother to respond. He could see that this was a feisty one and he wasn't in the mood for a shouting match. Instead, he held out his driver's license. "Here's my information," he said, his voice all business. "You can make a note while I grab my insurance papers." When she didn't take the card from his hand he rested it on the hood of his car then walked around to the passenger's side of the Maserati where he flipped open the glove compartment and grabbed his documents.

When he went back to the front of his car Miss Brave and Bold was bending over, examining the damage to her back bumper, giving him a pretty good view of her taut derriere. Nice.

As he got closer she straightened. "Not too bad. The bang sounded a lot worse than it looks." She gave him a bold stare then held out her driver's license to him. "Here. I'll go write your stuff down while you do mine." She dropped the card into his palm and stepped over to where he'd left his driver's license, her movements smooth and lithe like an athlete's.

Stone stared after her but she paid him no mind. Strange. His stares were known to set the ladies tittering. But not this one. It was obvious that she was not easily impressed or intimidated.

She picked up the card and stared at it for a couple of seconds. Then she lifted it closer to her face and a chuckle escaped her lips. Then it turned into an all-out laugh.

Stone scowled. It wasn't his best picture but, come on, it wasn't that bad. He stepped closer and stared at his driver's license in her long, lean fingers. "What's so funny?" he growled.

"Your...your name," she said, in between laughs. She turned her eyes on him and this time, instead of cutting anger, they were filled with dancing mirth. "Is your name really..." more laughter, "...Gladstone? You don't look like a Gladstone to me." And more laughter tumbled from her lips as she staggered back and leaned against the hood, clutching her chest in a fake laughter-induced heart attack.

His face grew as dark as his mood. The woman was laughing at him. "It's Stone," he said, his voice cold and hard. "Stone Hudson." No-one called him by his first name. Absolutely no-one. They knew better. Until this woman came along...

Still laughing, she nodded. "Okay, Gladstone...Stone, I got you." Then, still chuckling, she pushed up and off the hood and headed for her SUV, the card still in her hand.

Stone stayed where he was, still simmering, and as he watched her through the back glass he saw her pick up a pen and pull a small notepad from the bag on the passenger's seat. She began to write. And she was still chuckling.

Stone glared at the back of her head, feeling like he could happily wring her neck but, of course, he could not. Frustrated, he growled deep in his throat then looked down at the card in his hand. "Indiana Moon Lane", it read. And, like him, she had a Burlington address. Twenty-nine years old with a birthday coming up in a month. So he was right. She was four years his junior. And, like most driver's licenses, the picture didn't do her any justice. In the photo her hair was much longer, falling in a black curtain to her shoulders and her face looked thin. But those eyes could never be hidden. They jumped out at you, sharp as daggers, and that determined set of her mouth told anyone looking that she was a force to be reckoned with.

"Got everything you need?"

He looked up to see her standing beside him. How the heck had she done that? He hadn't heard a sound but there she was, right by his elbow.

"Just a sec." He reached through the window of his car and grabbed the novel he'd bought in the airport. Quickly, he copied her particulars into the back of the book and when she handed him her insurance papers he recorded that information as well. He turned around to hand them back to her but she had her back to him, her cell phone positioned as she took photos of her car.

"For the record," she said and gave him a smile that wasn't mocking or sarcastic but wide and genuine and beautiful, a smile that so transformed her face that he couldn't help but stare. Again.

For a moment they both stood there – he, staring at her and she, smiling at him. She almost looked like she wanted to say something else, probably even strike up a real conversation, nothing to do with cars or accidents. He certainly did.

But then, just as he was about to speak, she took the papers from him then stepped back and lifted her hand in a little wave. "Well, I've got to run," she said. "Got things to do and people to see. In fact," she glanced away and a look of concern flitted across her face, "I'd better get cracking on my next assignment, as crazy as it is."

Crazy assignment? That piqued his interest but he got no chance to ask questions. She was already walking back to her SUV.

Indiana Moon Lane slid into the driver's seat, started the vehicle, and without a backward glance she merged into the slow-moving traffic and was gone.

Stone, half bewildered, half intrigued, stared after her. This woman, so fearless and direct, was a world apart from the hothouse flowers he was used to. In fact, she looked like she'd be happier on the wide open plains of the wild west or the jungles of South America than stuck in the middle of traffic on a Canadian highway.

Then a thought came to him, a crazy thought, but he couldn't shake it. What if she was the one he'd been looking for all along?

CHAPTER TWO

Indie pushed the supermarket trolley down the aisle with Tessa in tow. She reached for a head of Romaine lettuce and threw it into the cart on top of the bag of potatoes, tray of sweet corn and the big green watermelon that she planned to devour later. She loved herself some watermelon.

She was bending over to grab a bag of navel oranges from a huge bin when Tessa grabbed her arm.

"What about that one?" her friend whispered fiercely.

Indie looked up and there, at the end of the aisle, was a very tall, very handsome man, his long dark hair pulled back with a string, his muscular arms quite visible in a sleeveless exercise top. He was wearing sweatpants and gym shoes and he had a carton of milk in his shopping basket. He was studying the label on a box of cereal. Obviously, a health nut. Not that that was a bad thing. But still...

"So?" Tessa nudged her. "What do you think?"

Indie grimaced and turned her attention back to the oranges. "Nah. Too pretty."

"Too pre-" Tessa glared up at her. "Will you be serious? You asked me to help you, Indie, but you're not even trying."

"I am serious. Too pretty." Indie looked down at her diminutive friend, her straight blonde hair falling past her shoulders, her big brown eyes and full red lips giving her the appearance of a cute little doll. Now that was the look men craved. Who would waste time looking at a short-haired Amazon like her when a little princess like

Tessa was right there? Indie sighed. "When will you learn, Tessa? Heartthrobs like that aren't looking for women like me. I'm too big and intimidating. Too plain. Now go hunt me somebody else more ordinary looking."

Indie dropped the oranges into the cart and moved on to the tomatoes but out of the corner of her eye she could see Tessa standing there in the aisle, glowering at her. Then, with a sigh of obvious frustration, she turned and headed down the cereal aisle.

Indie could only shake her head and smile. Once she set her mind to something, Tessa took it very seriously. Indie had left straight from the attorney's office and headed back to her car where she'd called her best friend from her cell phone. Once she'd shared her dilemma with Tessa, she'd taken it on as her own personal project, telling Indie to head straight home to Burlington so they could plan. Tessa was something else, always up for a challenge, especially when it involved men.

Indie left the vegetable aisle and was on her way to the bakery section when Tessa came flying toward her, all smiles. "I found him, Indie, and don't tell me you don't like him. I spoke to him and he's pleasant and smart. He's a high school math teacher. And he's ordinary looking, just like you asked."

Before Indie could say a word in response Tessa grabbed the trolley and began pushing it toward aisle seven.

"Hey, wait up."

Even with her little legs Tessa was moving fast and Indie had to hurry to catch up. "Listen," she whispered loudly to her friend's back, "I don't know if this is such a good idea, hunting men in the super-"

"Phillip! Hi. Fancy running into you again so quickly." Tessa pushed the trolley toward a man wearing dark slacks and a light blue dress shirt. At the sound of her voice he turned quickly, a broad smile on his face.

"Tessa." He looked genuinely happy to see her. "I thought I had lost you. One minute I was reaching for a box of cornflakes and the next moment you'd disappeared."

"Oh, I just went to get my friend," Tessa told him then she turned to Indie, looking as pleased as pie. Indie almost rolled her eyes.

"Phillip, I'd like you to meet my friend, Indiana Lane. Indie, this is Phillip Robertson." She reached out and grabbed Indie's hand, dragging her forward, almost making her bump into the man whose smile suddenly went stiff then slowly began to fade.

"Oh," he said and blinked then he looked from Indie to Tessa then back to Indie. Then he stuck out his hand. "Pleased to meet you, Ms. Lane."

Yeah, right. Indie knew it wasn't her he wanted to get to know, it was Tessa. When she'd struck up her conversation with him he must have been flattered, thinking she was interested in him. And then to be thrown a serious-looking, no makeup woman who was taller than he was? Obviously, not what he was expecting.

"Yes, good meeting you, too," Indie said and, just to be polite, she shook his hand. "Now, if you'll excuse me, I still have a lot of shopping to do."

It was almost funny to see the look of relief that passed over the man's face when he saw that she was leaving. Almost. She was a tough bird but what woman wanted to know that a man found her so unattractive that he was glad she was leaving? That was what she got for hanging out with Tessa. Sometimes it sucked to have such a pretty little friend hanging around. It highlighted just how unfeminine she was, with her tall frame, short hair and plain face. Crap.

She was pushing the trolley toward the frozen food section when Tessa came running after her. "Indie, are you insane? Why did you go running off like that? He was perfect."

"Yeah," she said with a snort. "With him being four inches shorter than me and bald, how could I give up such a catch? I must be freakin' crazy."

"Hey, there's no need to be sarcastic."

Indie groaned. "You're right. That was uncalled for and I'm sorry. But don't you see the guy was all ga-ga over you? It wasn't me he wanted."

"If you'd just given him a chance-"

"Look," Indie said, cutting Tessa off before she started to lecture her on a hopeless cause, "I know you're just trying to help. And I know this situation is absurd, what with that stupid deadline. But I don't think picking up men in the supermarket is the answer."

Tessa set her mouth in a pout and folded her arms across her chest. "So what do you suggest, Miss Smarty Pants? Do you have a man tucked away somewhere that I don't know about?"

Indie rolled her eyes. "You know I don't. Unless you count that aid worker who took a shine to me in Haiti."

Tessa burst out laughing. "You mean Gorilla George from New Orleans? From what you told me he's three times your size and twice your age."

"Yeah," Indie said with a shake of her head, "but he's available."

Tessa glared at her. "We're desperate but not that desperate." Then her look softened. "Don't you know anybody? What about an old boyfriend?"

"I don't have time for boyfriends."

"Which is exactly why we're in this situation right now," Tessa said, looking none too pleased. "You've got to make time for social life, Indie. Life's not just about saving the world. It's also about love, and family and kids-"

"Okay, stop right there. That's your idea of life, not mine."

"You're right." Tessa's shoulders fell and she stared off toward the cashier. Then, her mind obviously working overtime, she turned back to Indie, an excited look on her face. "I know exactly where to find men who want to get married."

Indie frowned. Nothing good ever happened when Tessa got that excited look.

"Where?"

"In a church, where else? Men of the cloth – not priests, of course – are always looking for good women to marry. And the men in the congregation, too, they're looking for wives, aren't they?" She began to push the trolley toward the cashier's counter. "Come on. We've got some church services to crash."

At that point Indie knew Tessa had finally gone off her rocker. "Stop."

That brought the little blonde dynamo to a halt. She looked back with an expression that said Indie was the one who had gone bonkers. She put her hands on her hips. "Okay, that's it. I've been the one coming up with all the ideas and you've killed every one of them. There's got to be even one man in this whole world who you like. Come on, woman. Give me something to work with. Anything."

That made Indie pause and think. One man who she liked...

"Well," she began, her voice uncertain, "there is one man..."

"Thank you, Jesus." Tessa raised her hands in an expression of praise then she ran to Indie. "So, who is it? Tell me who you like and I'll pull out all the stops to help you reel him in even before the thirty days are up. Who is he and where can I find him?"

"I remember his name," Indie said with a chuckle, "because it's real funny. Gladstone Hudson. Gladstone. Can you believe it?" She was grinning now. "Although he calls himself Stone so he can sound more macho. I have his address in my notebook. It's in the car."

Tessa frowned and cocked her head to one side. "Something's fishy here. It sounds like you hardly know this Gladstone fellow."

Indie shrugged. "Just met him today. In the car accident."

Tessa opened her eyes wide. "No. He's the one who ran into the back of your car this evening?"

"The same."

"And he's the one you like? But how do you know you like him? You spent all of ten minutes together."

Indie shrugged again. "All I know is, he's the only man I've ever met who made my heart race just at the sight of him." Then she laughed. "Of course, I never let on that he had any effect on me. I was cool as cucumber."

Tessa nodded as she stared at Indie. "I can bet." Then slowly her dazed look melted and the old Tessa was back. A mischievous grin tickled her lips. "Okay, Miss Indiana Moon Lane, let's get on home and start planning Operation Catch Mr. Gladstone Hudson right away."

And as she headed off to the cashier, pushing the trolley as she went, Indie could only shake her head and smile. With Tessa Tyndale on the case Stone Hudson was going to be in for a bumpy ride.

. . ❧ . .

"INDIANA MOON LANE." Stone said the name softly to himself as he stared down at the blank page on which he'd written the information. A day had passed since he'd run into her – literally – and he was just as intrigued now as he'd been when he first laid eyes on her.

And he was determined to see her again.

It wasn't just that he found her fascinating – her boldness, her exotic look, her name. For some reason he felt that their meeting, although not under the most ideal condition, was meant to be. For a long time he'd been looking for someone like Indiana Lane and just like that, when he hadn't even been looking, she'd fallen right into his lap. Of course, he had no idea if she would agree to work for him but he intended to make the proposal and do his best to convince her to come on board.

But first he had to call his project manager. Although it was just one-thirty in the afternoon in Ontario it was already seven-thirty in the evening in South Africa. He knew Jenna had already signed off for the evening and he hated calling her so late but she was so easygoing. She never complained. In fact, if he would be perfectly honest, she spoiled him.

Jenna picked up on the third ring. "Yeah, boss?"

Stone chuckled. "Didn't I tell you to stop calling me that?"

"Can't help it," she said, laughing into the phone. "I happen to enjoy teasing you. What can I help you with, Stone?"

"Good news. I've finally found the perfect person to replace you."

He heard Jenna's happy gasp then the words came tumbling out in a breathless stream. "Oh my Lord, that's great news. Who is it? When can he start? Or is it a she? Get them on the plane right away because this baby is not gonna wait-"

"Hold on, not so fast." He practically had to shout to get the words in above hers. "It's a her and I haven't hired her yet."

Silence on the other end of the line. A full five seconds passed before Jenna spoke again. "What do you mean you haven't hired her yet?" Then, before Stone could respond she continued. "Oh, you've done the interviews but you just haven't told her she's hired."

"No," he said, dragging out the word. In her state he didn't want to give her too many shocks. "I haven't actually asked her yet."

"What? Stone, I'm going to have this baby any day now. You need to find me a replacement. Like yesterday!"

"I know, Jenna." He rubbed the back of his neck. Damn him for being such a perfectionist. There were so many other people he could have hired to cover for Jenna but no, he had to find the perfect one. And it had taken him this long to identify her. He'd be up the creek if he reached out to Indiana Lane and she said no.

"Don't you worry your little head," he said, his voice sounding a whole lot more confident than he felt. "I'll be back on a plane to South Africa in no time and I'll have your replacement with me."

CHAPTER THREE

"**O**h... my...gosh." Tessa stared at the computer screen, her mouth falling open. "Oh my gosh, oh my gosh."

"What?" Indie gave her a stony-eyed look. Tessa, ever the drama queen, was famous for getting all excited over nothing at all.

"Come here, Indie. Come look at this." Her eyes glued to the screen, Tessa waved Indie over. "You've got to see this."

In no hurry at all, Indie laid down the list she'd been working on – a list of tactics to snag Stone Hudson, no less – and got up from the armchair then walked over to the computer desk where Tessa perched on the edge of the rolling office chair. If she wasn't careful, that thing would roll back and she'd find herself flat on her face.

Indie pushed Tessa's chair closer to the desk and set her foot behind the wheel so it wouldn't run back. Just one more thing in her constant task of keeping her accident-prone friend out of danger. "What's up?" she asked, as she bent down to see the screen.

Tessa reached out and turned the screen so that Indie could have a better view. "Is this the guy who ran into you?"

Indie leaned forward. "Yeah. Is he a criminal or something?"

"Did you know," Tessa said in a voice rising higher with each word, "that Stone Hudson is the owner of Hudson Broadcasting Corporation?"

Indie jerked upright then fixed her friend with a narrowed gaze. "Get outta here." Tessa was a flighty one but this story took the cake.

"No, it's true," she said, her eyes wide. "Look."

As she pointed to the screen Indie's eyes followed her finger. Wikipedia. And the heading read. "Gladstone 'Stone' Hudson, chairman and CEO, Hudson Broadcasting Corporation". And there, staring back at her, was the face of the man she was busily planning to catch.

"Well, hot damn." The words escaped her in a whisper that was breathless with disbelief. Who would have thought...

"You know, we should have put two and two together," Tessa said, still staring at the screen. "I've heard the name Stone Hudson before. Why didn't it come to me that it could be him?"

Indie gave a snort. "Probably because you wouldn't think that, of all the people in the world, it would be a billionaire who would slam into my car. How many billionaires do you know?"

"None."

"Me neither. And that's why you wouldn't expect..." Indie's voice trailed off as another thought came to her. "Now that I think of it, his car seemed pretty darned expensive. All black, sports car type, with a funny-looking symbol like a crown with three points."

Tessa gave her an incredulous stare. "A trident?"

"Yeah, that's it."

"A Maserati," Tessa said with a gasp. "He ran into you with his Maserati. Do you have any idea how much those cars cost?"

Indie shrugged.

"You're looking at about two hundred thousand, easy."

"Good to know." Indie folded her arms across her chest and nodded, momentarily lost in thought. Then, with a sigh of resignation, she walked back to the armchair and picked up her list. She walked over to the garbage can in the corner and began to rip the paper, dropping the slivers into the bin.

"Well," she said with a wry smile, "there goes Plan A."

Tessa whipped around and stared at her. "What are you doing?"

"Getting rid of my list of ways to attract Stone Hudson. It was hard enough coming up with ideas to catch a regular guy. What hope would I have with a billionaire?"

"Are you crazy, Indie? He's the only man you like and he's single. We have to keep going."

Indie shook her head. "That's where you and I are different, Tessa. You're a dreamer. I'm practical. And I know I don't have the chance of a snowball in Hades with a man like Stone Hudson. Heck, I probably wouldn't have a chance with him even if he were a regular guy. Who am I kidding?" She dropped the last scrap of paper into the bin, patted her hands together in finality then walked back to the armchair where she flopped down.

So much for finding a man in thirty days. Correction – twenty-nine. She might as well practice pursing her lips so she'd be ready when it was time to kiss the fourteen million dollars goodbye. Oh, well...

"Indiana Moon Lane, I can't believe you, the great granddaughter of a Mohawk Chief, are behaving like this. Shame on you." Tessa marched over to where Indie sat, pretty much ignoring her, and swatted her on the arm.

"Hey, you." Indie jerked back and rubbed the wounded limb. "Settle down, squirt."

"I will," Tessa said in a huff, "as soon as you get your act together and we start planning again. Now, it's..." she glanced at the clock on the wall, "...three minutes before two and we have to figure out a way to reach this man before the day is out. We need to get an appointment and fast."

"All right." Indie got up and strolled over to the desk. She picked up the phone. "You want an appointment, I'll get an appointment. Where we go from there, that's anybody's guess." She flipped open her notebook with Stone's number, picked up the phone and dialed. It began to ring and she held her breath.

"Hello." His voice was the same deep mellow timbre she remembered from the day before. It sent a delicious shiver up her spine.

Indie grimaced. This was not the time to turn into a girly girl, swooning at the sound of a man's voice. She was above that sort of thing. Upset with herself, she spoke through clenched teeth. "This is Indie Lane," she began then realizing she was sounding angry and, of course, he wouldn't understand why, she released her breath, forcing herself to relax. "This is Indie," she said again. "We met yesterday-"

"Yes, of course," he said, his voice carrying a hint of surprise. "Indiana Moon lane. I was just about to call you."

That made Indie straighten up. "You were?"

"Yes. But I cut you off. What were you calling about?"

"No, you go ahead," Indie said quickly. Maybe he had a good reason to call her. Right now her reason for calling him seemed just a little bit lame. *I'd like an appointment with you to see how I can trap you into marriage.* He'd call for the straitjacket right away.

"I wonder if you would meet with me tomorrow to discuss a possible opportunity...if you're interested, that is." He cleared his throat. "Of course, I don't know your situation but I'm looking for a project manager to take over the operations of a charity I run in South Africa. You struck me as the right person for the job."

"Oh, is that right?" Indie couldn't keep a touch of sarcasm out of her voice. Why had he thought that? Because she looked strong and tough...for a woman?

"There's an aura about you," he said, "something I can't explain. All I can say is, I sense that you'll love those orphans and give them the affection only a true loving spirit can."

Orphans. He'd said orphans. And if there was one thing that pulled her heartstrings and made her spring into action it was the opportunity to make a difference in the lives of orphaned kids. Stone Hudson had read her like a wide-open book – after just one very brief meeting.

"I'd love to hear more," she said.

He responded with a laugh. "I knew you would. Now the only question is, how soon can we meet? The situation is a bit urgent, I'm afraid. My current project manager is due to have a baby soon. Would you be available tomorrow?"

Indie bit her lip. Tomorrow was good but today was even better. The sooner she could get a face-to-face meeting with Stone the sooner she could start working her plan...or, more accurately, Tessa's. They didn't have much time. "What about today?"

"Sounds good to me," he said without hesitation. "The sooner, the better."

"Is five o'clock too late? I could be at your office by then." Indie was feeling pleased with herself at how easily she'd pulled off an early meeting when she looked over and saw Tessa. Her friend was frantically shaking her head and mouthing the word 'later'.

"Wait, five o'clock may not work. What about seven?" Indie backtracked but meanwhile she was glaring at Tessa. What was wrong with her?

"We could meet at Palmetto's, that great restaurant on Maple Avenue."

"That's fine," Indie said, feeling totally distracted. Tessa was signaling something else and she couldn't figure out what two fingers pointing to the lips meant. She was so preoccupied with Tessa, if Stone had suggested they meet under a bridge she would have agreed. "I'll see you at seven," she said then hung up.

"What?" She gave Tessa a look of annoyance. "Didn't you see I was trying to set up the appointment?"

"Yes, and that's the problem."

Indie narrowed her gaze. "The problem? I thought that was the plan."

"It was at first but then I thought, why settle for an appointment when you can get a date?" Tessa gave her a grin of triumph. "And it worked! Now we have exactly five hours to get you ready." She ran over and grabbed Indie's arm. "Come on."

"Where are we going?" Indie pulled back, unwilling to get caught up in Tessa's whirlwind of excitement.

"To the mall, of course. We have to get you a dress, shoes, a nice purse, makeup. Oh, and your hair. We've got to do something about that hair."

Indie lifted her hand and ran her fingers through her black strands. "What's wrong with it?"

Tessa rolled her eyes. "You're seriously asking that question? It makes you look like a boy. Now once my hair stylist gets his hands on you, you'll be a new woman. He'll layer the strands, get your hair to softly frame your face and soften those lines, then he'll-"

"All right, whatever." Indie grabbed her keys from off the desk and stuffed them into her pocket. "Let's go."

Tessa almost bounced out of the room, she was so eager.

Indie could only sigh. For years Tessa had been trying to 'beautify' her with manicured nails, fancy dresses and jewelry. She'd resisted every attempt until now. But fate – or maybe just her desire to get the fourteen million dollars – had led her straight into Tessa's hands. Heaven help her.

They jumped into the Land Rover and sped off to The Burlington Mall where Tessa took Indie on a whirlwind shopping spree, dragging her into at least eight stores until they found the perfect dress, an emerald green sheath that showed off her long legs and svelte frame. Then, a quick dash to Julio's, where the expert trimmed and feathered until Indie's hair caressed her nape, emphasizing her slender neck and tickling her cheeks. When he spun the chair around so she could look in the mirror she almost didn't recognize herself. If she should admit it, she could actually pass for a beautiful woman. A model, even. When Tessa said Julio had talent and could transform her, she wasn't kidding.

"Now for the shoes." Tessa dragged her off again, and this time it took three shoe stores before they found a pretty pair that made Indie's size nine feet look dainty.

An eyebrow and upper lip wax and a manicure later, Indie was out of pocket a few hundred dollars but actually quite pleased with her new look. It was a far cry from the rugged, outdoorsy look she usually sported.

"It's a quarter to six," Tessa said, pointing to the clock on the salon wall. "We've got to get you ready."

It took them exactly eighteen minutes to get to Indie's house which was thankfully only three blocks away from Tessa's. At least she wouldn't have to drop her friend home before rushing off to her date. Tessa could easily walk. It took Indie another twenty minutes to shower and dress and twelve whole minutes for Tessa to do her makeup. Indie had thought the haircut was transforming but when Tessa was done she could truly say she was a new woman. *Move over, Lois Lane. Indiana Lane is ready to snag herself her own Superman.*

At the door she drew in a deep breath, tucked her gold purse under her arm and gave Tessa a slightly less than confident smile. "Wish me luck," she whispered, not feeling at all like her usual self-assured self but more like the wishy-washy women she normally scoffed at. Now, with her mission being to capture the full attention of her target, she had become one of them. Her lips curled in self derision. The things people did for money. Although, in her case it would all go to worthy causes. She didn't intend to spend a cent of it on herself. That is, assuming she even got it...

But even as she walked to her vehicle Indie knew deep down that this wasn't all about the money. To her chagrin she was beginning to realize that there was a part of her that really wanted this – the date, getting to know Stone Hudson and maybe, just maybe, getting him to feel something for her, possibly attraction, maybe even...love.

She shook her head. *Get your mind out of the clouds, woman. This is business.* She started the engine and pulled out of the driveway then headed off to her date with Stone Hudson. With her purse full of notes from Tessa, instructions on how to mesmerize the man in question, the night promised to be interesting, to say the least.

CHAPTER FOUR

Stone strode into Palmetto's where he was a well-known and valued patron. He was immediately ushered to the private lounge reserved for special guests. He'd left instructions for Indiana to be escorted to this private dining room immediately upon arrival. He hated to keep a lady waiting and had made sure to get there over ten minutes earlier than the appointed time.

He was relaxed in the plush chair, skimming the wine list, when the maitre-d' ushered in an exquisitely elegant lady in a stunning emerald dress that molded her curves like a second skin. As the man brought her closer Stone raised his eyebrows in surprise. Why was she here? Had they got his unexpected visitor mixed up with someone else?

He rose to his feet and gave a courteous nod and that was when he got a really good look at the queen who had sauntered into his private salon. Her lips pert and prettily painted, her hair soft and feathery around her face and her eyes – those beautiful eyes, now arresting in their beauty, the colors on the lids making them sparkling green behind her long lashes. The regal beauty standing before him was none other than his awaited guest, Indiana Lane.

Her dramatic beauty stunned Stone. He knew Indiana was beautiful but this was way beyond what he could have imagined. Realizing he was still staring he gave her a smile to break the tension.

She smiled back then she did something that threw him for a loop. Was she batting her eyelids at him? He had to stop himself before he got caught in a frown. Was cool and matter-of-fact Indiana Lane flirting with him?

He had no time to ponder that question. She was standing right in front of him now, her lips parted, her chin tilted up toward him.

"Indiana, thank you for coming," he said as his eyes roamed her face. "You look very beautiful this evening."

She cocked her eyebrow and gave him a slow, even smile. "Why, thank you," she breathed, her voice a deep, sultry purr.

God, what a contrast to the firm tone she'd used on him the evening before. He blinked then pulled out the chair for her and as she sat down his nostrils were filled with the seductive fragrance of her perfume. He could only describe it as seductive because, if the tightness in his groin was anything to go by, he had already fallen under her spell.

He went to sit on his own chair, thankful for the chance to hide his lower half from view. With relief he took the wine list from the maitre d' and pretended to be lost in its contents. He needed those few seconds to readjust his thermostat. He put a hand up and ran his finger inside his collar then tugged his tie back in place. God, it was hot in here.

The maitre d' called a black-suited young man and thankfully, by the time the server took the orders, Stone was back to normal. The room had cooled down wonderfully in the past few minutes.

He turned round from thanking the server and was just about to say something charming to Indiana – or 'Indie' as she called herself – when he noticed that she'd opened her little gold purse and was carefully perusing what looked like a folded sheet of paper on which she had notes or some sort of list. And as she read she was frowning, seeming deep in concentration, and she was mouthing the words. If he could read lips he would swear she'd mouthed, "Always flatter him". He almost laughed at his stupidity. There was no way her paper said anything like that. He was ninety-nine percent sure that what she was reading had something to do with business.

"Lots of things on your 'To-Do' list?" he said with a smile. "Had to take you work with you, I see." His tone was teasing. He knew what it was to have a million and one things to cram into a measly twenty-four hours.

Indie jumped and her wide-eyed gaze flew to his. She immediately dropped her gaze again, shoved the paper back into her purse and snapped it shut. Then she dragged it off the table and dropped it onto her lap. When she looked up again her face was rosy with a guilty blush.

That only made Stone smile wider. It was amusing, maybe even sweet, that she'd taken her work with her and then felt guilty at being caught. "It's okay," he said magnanimously. "No need to feel bad. I've been guilty of the same thing."

When she gave him a look of confusion he continued. "Taking my work with me. Not leaving it back at the office."

At that, her face cleared. "Oh," she said, a look of relief passing over her face, "that. Yes, I...can't seem to leave the office behind." She gave a little giggle and it made her seem much younger and a whole lot less audacious than the woman he'd met the day before. Charming, but he sort of missed the woman he'd run into.

By the time the meal arrived Indie was almost back to what he considered her normal self, ribbing him again about his name. She was never going to let him live that one down. But then, just like the transformation that had taken place with her appearance, her personality changed again. Indie's lips softened in a smile and her eyelids lowered seductively. "Uhm, that's a lovely tie you're wearing."

Stone couldn't even remember which tie he'd grabbed when he was getting dressed. He glanced down and saw that it was a narrow black one with thin, almost invisible strips of gray. Nothing spectacular, as far as he was concerned. But maybe it appealed to women. He had no idea, but Indie certainly seemed to like it. "Thank you." He acknowledged her compliment with a nod and a smile.

"And your cologne," she said softly. "What is it? Issey Miyake?"

Surprised, he nodded. She had a great nose for scents.

"Perfect choice," she almost crooned. "It suits you." Then she lifted her glass and the tip of her pink tongue slipped from between ruby lips to taste the dark red liquid. She took a slow sip and raised shimmering green eyes to him.

Stone almost groaned. If she kept this up he'd probably reach across the table for her and kiss her senseless. A man could only take so much. He shifted in his seat but getting comfortable was next to impossible just then.

He cleared his throat. "How's your steak?" he asked as he picked up his fork again.

She blinked. Then, as if snapping out of a trance, she straightened up and the smoldering embers left her eyes. Instead, the mischievous light was back and her lips curled in a smile. "Very well done, like I asked."

He looked at the dark mass on her plate. "It looks like it's been burned to a crisp," he said.

"Just the way I like it," she said with a laugh and to his relief it was a real laugh, not low and sexy and disturbing, but light and melodic and genuine. Now that was the Indie he liked.

After that, they settled into companionable conversation while they ate until Indie closed her knife and fork and dabbed at her lips with her napkin. "I'll be right back," she said, smiling. "I just need to powder my nose."

Gracefully, she got up and turned to go but then she spun around and grabbed her tiny purse from where she'd placed it beside her napkin. Another bright smile and then she was walking away, her hips swaying with every step.

She was almost at the door, heading out of the private dining room, when the seductive sway of her hips was interrupted by a stumble and then a curse under her breath. Stone made to get up and help her but she immediately righted herself and, still muttering, disappeared through the door.

He sank back in his chair, shaking his head. Talk about a mystery woman. One minute alluring temptress and the next, swearing like a truck driver, albeit under her breath. Which one was she, really? No wonder men could never understand women. With a man, what you saw was pretty much what you got. With a woman, you just never knew...

Stone was still pondering the enigma that was Indiana Lane when she returned. And just like before, he had to do a double take. Where was the siren who had just left the table?

Indie was approaching but this was a different Indie from the one who had arrived at the restaurant over an hour earlier. The gold eye shadow was gone and so was the pink blush that had highlighted her already lovely cheekbones. And the ruby lips she'd pursed and pouted earlier? Gone. In their place were the soft pink lips that had chastised him the evening before.

When Indie got to the table she didn't even give him a chance to get up and pull out the chair for her. Cheeks flushed, she sat down and dropped her purse on top of the table. She let out a deep sigh. "I can't do this. It's just not me."

He smiled and leaned forward. "What? The makeup?"

"Yes," she said, giving him a crooked grin. "And the high heels. I was trying to make a good first impression...or second...but my face felt like some kid had plastered watercolor paints all over it. And not to mention these darned high heels." She chuckled. "Not exactly everyday wear for me. Let's just say it's been a while since I had to fit myself out in this kind of get-up." She gave him a rueful smile. "Sorry."

That made him laugh. "I'm not. I'm glad the old Indie is back. She's the one I want to talk to. As beautiful as she maybe, I don't think a fashion pot can do the job I have in mind."

Then it was her turn to laugh and her eyes sparkled with amusement. "Fashion pot? Who the hell says 'fashion pot'?" Then she put her hands to her lips. "Oops, sorry," she said, but she didn't look sorry at all. "I meant 'who the heck.'"

Serious as a judge, he replied, "Yes, of course you did."

Then they both ended up laughing and with that the tension was broken and they relaxed.

"Indie," Stone said, "as I mentioned to you, I would love it if you could join my team in South Africa. I've adopted an orphanage there. It has nothing to do with Hudson Broadcasting Corporation. This is a personal project of mine."

"I love the idea already," she said, her face eager. "When can I start?"

Stone sat back, surprised. "When can you start? That sounds like you're available right away."

"I am." She spoke without hesitation.

Wow, could he be so lucky? She hadn't required any convincing at all.

"My only question is…"

Stone held his breath, knowing an objection was coming next. It had been too easy, of course. There had to be an issue somewhere.

"…will you be there, too, at the orphanage? Or will I be heading out there on my own?" She looked him straight in the eyes. "Because the only way I'll take the job is if you come to South Africa with me. At least, for the start."

"Well, I did plan to go with you and get you established," he said, rubbing his chin, "probably stay a couple of weeks until you're comfortable. But then I'd have to head back-"

"Deal. That sounds like a plan to me." She sat back in her chair, a look of satisfaction on her face.

Well, that was easy. They hadn't even discussed remuneration or benefits but already she was accepting the offer, accepting a position she didn't even have the full details on. Her only concern seemed to be whether he'd be there at the start or not. All his hiring should be this easy.

There was something about the whole thing that puzzled him, though. She didn't strike him as the fearful, dependent type. In fact, it was her air of independence and decisiveness that had drawn him to her. Why, then, did she insist that he go with her? It just did not add up.

And then there was the fact that she'd been so available. Immediately. Not that he minded. Like Jenna had said, he needed her like yesterday. But didn't she have a family or obligations? He hadn't seen a ring so he guessed she wasn't married and probably didn't have kids but she had to have parents. She would certainly want to see them before leaving for a country so far away. And what about...a boyfriend?

"Now it's my turn to ask you a question," he said, and although he was dreading the answer he plunged right in. "Aren't there people you need to say goodbye to? Your parents or...anyone else?"

"Nope," she said, her voice firm in its finality. "Don't have any parents, don't have any pets, and don't have a boyfriend."

Well, that answered that. The boyfriend part at least. But no parents? "Forgive me for asking but...did your parents pass away?"

"My mom died," she said, her face gone thoughtful and her voice quiet. "And my dad, well, let's just say he's been missing in action since I was three. That's when my parents got divorced. I haven't seen or heard from him since the day he moved out."

Stone frowned. A deadbeat dad. No wonder Indie seemed so strong and self-sufficient. She'd had to be, surviving without a father. She'd probably had to fight her own battles all her life.

"Sorry to hear that." What he was saying was inadequate but he couldn't think of anything else that would show her that, to the extent that he could understand her life, he felt her pain.

She shrugged. "That's okay. It was the best thing he ever did for us, walking out like that. At least I didn't have to watch my mom crouching by the wall with blows raining down on her. Damned alcoholics." She spat the words out in disgust.

Stone was feeling disgust, too – at himself. He'd gone and stirred up all sorts of bad memories with his stupid questions. The cross examination would end right here. He'd done enough damage for one night.

"Be ready to fly out day after tomorrow," he said. As she opened her mouth to speak he put up a hand, stopping her. "I know you're available as early as tomorrow but I need a day to tie up some loose ends before I move again. And besides," he said, "you need the day to get your police record and drop into the clinic to get your shots."

"Oh." Her face fell. "Forgot about that."

"There's no great rush," he said, trying to reassure her. "The day after tomorrow will be good enough for me. A lot earlier than I expected, actually. I thought you would tell me you'd need at least a few weeks to get ready for such a move. To tell the truth," he shook his head, "I'm in shock. Your being ready to move right away seems almost too good to be true."

For some reason that made her look flustered. "Oh, it's just lucky timing, I guess." She shrugged. "Maybe it's fate."

Stone chuckled. He could believe that. Everything was falling into place so easily for him, the stars must be lined up just right. And he wasn't complaining.

Around a half hour later, after they'd gone through the details of the job, Stone walked Indie to her vehicle. As she turned toward him he looked down at her, at the lips that looked so soft and inviting. He kept that thought to himself. This had been a business meeting and he'd best remember that.

He put out his hand to her. "Thank you for agreeing to work with me on such short notice," he said. "I really appreciate it."

She looked down then slid her hand into his. Her fingers were warm, her handshake firm, and again that comfortable feeling flowed through him. This was a woman he could trust.

She jumped into the Land Rover and just like last time she gave him a wave. "See you in a couple of days." Then she was off.

As she drove out of the parking lot he stood there staring after her. If Indie's chameleon act was anything to go by, this trip to South Africa promised to be an interesting one. He was looking forward to what this mystery woman would do next.

CHAPTER FIVE

"You have to find lots of opportunities to catch him alone." Tessa's eyes twinkled with excitement. "If you can't find opportunities, create them. Just do anything you can to get him alone with you."

Skeptical, Indie shook her head. "I'll do my best but there's just so much you can do in four weeks. No, three and a half."

"Just use the strategies I gave you," Tessa pressed her.

"Yeah, like last time?" Indie grimaced. "I almost broke my behind walking in those high heels you put me in. It was darned embarrassing, too."

"This is different, Indie. This time I'm not going to try to make you into something you're not. No more makeup or high heels, I promise. You just have to remember these three little things." She went and sat on the bed next to Indie, her face earnest. "If a girl wants to snag a man in the shortest possible time she has to use frequent proximity, inviting body language and attitude."

Indie leaned back against the headboard and stared at her friend. "I get the frequent proximity and the body language part," she said as she folded her arms across her chest, "but give me that attitude part again. I thought I had more than enough of that."

"You're not listening, Indie." Tessa punched the bed with her fist. "I'm going to explain this one more time and you'd better listen because I'm not going through it again." She scowled at Indie. "I swear, whenever I speak you have a filter in your head that holds on to some of the stuff and the rest, it just leaves by the wayside."

Indie smiled at her sheepishly. Tessa was right. Half of the stuff she said, she didn't listen to anyway. It wasn't that she didn't want to. It was just that if you absorbed all of Tessa's chatter your head would explode. "Okay, okay," she said, releasing her arms and putting her hands up to defend herself from Tessa's wrath. The girl had been known to punch with very little provocation and a punch on the arm from that little fist could leave you in pain for days. "I'm listening now. Give it to me again."

Tessa heaved a sigh. "Okay, one more time. When I talk about attitude I mean that you should carry yourself like a princess. Never ask yourself if you're worthy of him. Ask if he's worthy of you."

"Okay." Indie drew out the word which made her sound doubtful which, of course, she was.

"Let him know he's the one who'll have to work for your favor. Let him do the chasing. And never, ever, come across as desperate."

Indie cocked an eyebrow. "Even though I am?"

Tessa sighed. "Yes, Indie, even though you are." She touched her friend's arm. "The fastest way to send a man running is to let him know how badly you want him."

"Got it," Indie said and hopped off the bed. "Now come help me finish packing." Then she grinned. "If all goes well, the next time you see me I'll be a married woman."

"That's the plan." Tessa grinned back and slid off the bed. Then her face went thoughtful. "One more thing. Please be helpless every once in a while. I know you always love to do everything by yourself but men love to help a maiden in distress. It makes them feel manly."

Indie straightened from where she'd been digging in her suitcase. She held up her hand. "One maiden in distress, coming up."

"Indie, I'm serious." Tessa swatted at her. "You joke around about everything."

"All right, all right, I'll try to be more helpless if you want. I pledge to do everything in my power to charm this man, even if it means acting like a wimp."

"Good. Remember, this is not for you. It's for the clinic you plan to build in Haiti, and the home in-"

"Got it, Tessa. I said I'm going to give it my best shot and I will. Now come and help me pack before I have to throw you out of my house."

Next day at the airport it was an emotional Tessa who hugged and kissed Indie goodbye.

"What are you crying about?" Indie asked as she hugged her close. "It's not like I don't go off on these far away trips every few months. This one is no different."

"I know," Tessa said, "but you've never gone so far away before. It's like the other side of the world."

"I'll be back in no time. You'll see."

They gave each other one last hug then Indie pulled away and headed off toward her gate. At the security check point she turned to give Tessa one last wave and then she went toward the security guard beckoning to her to proceed.

She always hated this part, when Tessa dropped her off. Like her, Tessa was an only child and they'd come to value their friendship so much that they were more like sisters than friends. Which was the amazing thing because they were so different in both looks and personality. But from the day they'd met four years ago something had clicked and they'd been a big part of each other's lives since then.

Indie collected her shoes from the bin, put them on then gathered up her carry-on items and headed for her gate. She had a whole hour to spare before boarding time and she planned to use it to catch up on her reading. It seemed that these days the only time she could find the time to engage in that favorite hobby was when she was sitting in an airport. She headed for the lounge where she'd wait for the boarding of Stone's private jet.

She was absorbed in a nail-biting scene in her suspense novel when she felt a weight on her shoulder. She jumped then looked up and there was Stone, smiling down at her.

He lifted his hand from her shoulder. "Sorry to startle you." He dropped his garment bag on an empty seat then relaxed onto the chair across from her.

"Wake me when the pilot calls us," he said with a groan. "I've had a long day." It certainly looked like he had. Within seconds he was breathing deeply, obviously dead to the world.

Indie raised her eyebrows. And she'd thought she'd been busy these last two days, getting ready for the trip. But if Stone's plunge into slumber was anything to go by, he'd had a heck of a rough time since she'd last seen him.

Slowly, she rested her novel down and leaned forward to peer at the sleeping man. She might as well do it now, get to know every inch of his face. She guessed that normally it would take at least three dates to be able to memorize a face down to the last detail. She didn't have the luxury of leisurely 'getting-to-know-you' dates so she would take advantage of the opportunity she'd been given and absorb every detail while she could.

She slid off her seat and slipped into the one beside him. Then, trying not to seem too obvious in case anyone walked in, as casually as she could she rested her chin in the hand she'd propped up on her knee and leaned over for a better look.

Stone Hudson wasn't a man you'd call eye candy. For one thing, his jaw was too firm for that description. And his forehead was too broad and strong. And his lips? Too tight. But there was a manliness about him that could not be denied. When you looked at him you knew that this was a man who was no walk-over. He was the kind of man who would defend his woman, protect her, be a source of strength for her. Indie gave a little smile. She liked that.

She was still smiling when Stone's eyes opened and he looked straight at her.

Indie jerked away and pressed back into the seat. Then she stole a sideways glance and saw that Stone was laughing at her.

He began to straighten up. "Was I snoring?" he asked with a rueful smile. "Don't tell me I was so loud you couldn't get any reading done."

"Not at all." Indie shook her head. "You were quiet as a mouse. I just thought I saw a...mosquito or something. I didn't want you to get stung."

He gave her a slow smile. "Thanks for looking out for me."

"No problem at all," she replied then she escaped back to her seat across the aisle, picked up her novel and sought refuge behind it. That was a close one. She'd better watch herself from here on. Few people took kindly to being stared at. She should know. She hated it herself.

Indie kept a low profile until they boarded the plane and even then she tried to keep a safe distance between her and Stone, making sure there was a seat that separated the two of them and reaching for a magazine she could hide behind. But then she remembered the real reason she was there – to attract this man, get him to want her so much that he would ask her to marry him. So far she'd been doing the exact opposite. She definitely had to work on her alluring side.

She dropped the magazine onto the middle seat and looked over to where Stone was peering at the screen of his laptop. She'd pretty much ignored the man since takeoff but now she would repair that. They had almost a day's worth of travel ahead of them so what better time to get to know him? Proximity, Tessa had said. She'd certainly have lots of that, stuck in a plane with Stone for the next several hours.

She cleared her throat and he looked up immediately. "Sorry," she said, giving him an apologetic smile, "I didn't mean to disturb you." Of course she'd meant to disturb him. She knew that and he knew that but it was the polite thing to say.

"Not at all," he said and pushed the laptop onto the nearby counter. "Are you okay?"

"I'm fine. Just a bit...bored."

Stone laughed. "What? With all the entertainment on the plane? You've got your choice of newspapers, magazines, music, movies and, my favorite, video games."

"You've got video games? Point me to them." Then she chuckled. "Just kidding. If you don't mind," her laughter softened to a smile, "I'd prefer talking to you. I mean, isn't it weird that I'm working for you now and I don't know that much about you?"

He shrugged. "Not weird at all. I have lots of employees I've never even met. But you're right. It makes sense for us to get more acquainted. What do you want to know?"

"Well, for one, what made you get involved with an orphanage all the way in South Africa? Are you in some kind of competition with Oprah? She built a school for girls and you decide to take on the boys?"

Stone's lips twitched with amusement. "Nothing like that. Oprah's in a class by herself. For me, it all started two years ago when I visited the country to launch Hudson Broadcasting Corporation in Johannesburg. I met a little boy, Moekebi Okechuckwu, a bright and shining star on the South African landscape..." as his voice trailed off his face looked thoughtful, "...and he was dying of AIDS."

"Oh, no." A familiar pain gripped Indie's heart. Since leaving university her whole life had been dedicated to working with children just like Moekebi. And no matter how many little ones you held in your arms while they made their finally journey to the next life, you never got used to it. Each case was a fresh, new heartache. She had a pretty good idea what Stone must be feeling right now.

"But that wasn't the worst part," Stone said, his eyes going back to her. "He was leaving behind a little brother who was only six years old and a sister who was only two. At twelve, he'd been both mother and father to these little ones."

"Their parents?"

"Already dead from the disease." Stone was silent for a moment then he spoke, and his voice was filled with the determination and hope now reflected on his face. "It seems like a daunting task, taking on the problems of a nation, but then I thought, no matter how small, doing a little is better than doing nothing at all." He shifted slightly in his seat, turning toward her. "Before he died I promised Moekebi I would take care of his little brother and sister. He died whispering my promise. That means a lot to me."

"And the children, they're at the orphanage now?"

"No, they live in a home just outside Johannesburg. I hired a home mother to care for them. She provides me with regular updates on their progress. Little Someleve just started kindergarten and Botuli is in the second grade."

Indie cocked her head to one side. "So how does the orphanage fit into this picture?"

"Here's the thing. Once I'd decided to help one family I felt I had to do more. Then, as if by some predetermined destiny, one of my South African employees mentioned the orphanage. It had fallen into severe disrepair. The orphans often had nothing to eat."

"But, how is that?" Indie frowned. "What about the social services?"

"This wasn't a government institution. It had been run by missionaries who, for whatever reason, packed up and returned to their countries. My best guess is that it was due to lack of funding."

Indie gave him a genuine smile of gratitude. She'd long since given up on any attempt at being flirtatious. In fact, she'd almost forgotten about that part of the plan. Rather than trying to tempt him, her smile meant she was truly interested in his story. "And that was when you stepped in."

He nodded. "Correct. That gift fell into my lap and I snapped it right up. And never felt better."

Indie shook her head in admiration. Who would have thought a Canadian billionaire would find so much joy in helping others so far away? "I can see that for you it's more than just giving money to a worthy cause. You're actually involved in what goes on in those kids' lives, aren't you?"

"I try to be, as much as I can. That's why I didn't mind the excuse to head back to South Africa to get you settled. I'll introduce you to each one of them. We have sixty boys in the home."

"A good number," Indie said, nodding. She was going to have her hands full but she was up for the challenge. Then as she looked over at him her curiosity got the better of her. "You've done a great job in creating a surrogate family but what about a family of your own? Is that something...you want to do?"

Then, just in case he thought she was zany to ask such a personal question she leaned back and put up her hand. "Just curious."

He gave her an unfathomable look then tightened his lips. "I was looking forward to having a family once. It didn't work out."

"I'm...sorry to hear that." Now she was really curious but there was no way she could dig deeper without coming off as rude. She gazed over at him, hoping he would continue but, typical male, that was where he shut up. Just when things sounded interesting.

"Yeah, life." He shrugged. "I learned my lesson. Walk cautiously in life, especially when making huge decisions. Some people are just not what they seem to be." He gave a grunt of what must have been disgust because on his face was a pained expression.

Interesting-er and interesting-er. So he'd been hurt...or betrayed...by a woman. That much she could guess from what he'd said.

And here she was, trying to trap him into the very thing he seemed bent on avoiding.

But hers was for a worthy cause, she reasoned. And besides, there was no denying she was genuinely attracted to him. And the more she learned about him, the more she liked him.

But the man was obviously suffering from the emotional bruises of a past relationship. So how in the world was she going to get him to fall in love with her now?

CHAPTER SIX

Twenty-five days to the deadline and Indie still had a long way to go in getting Stone Hudson to fall in love with her.

After the longest airplane journey she'd ever undertaken they'd rested at one of the grandest hotels in the city then a chauffeur wearing khakis came to pick them up in a Jeep Wrangler that looked perfect for the rugged terrain.

Stone was casually dressed today looking like an outdoors man in army-green slacks, khaki-collared shirt rolled up to the elbows, and boots. Indie couldn't help staring, maybe for a few seconds longer than she should have. She liked this rugged look of his. It was how she'd pictured him from the first day they'd met – big and tall and imposing against a wild landscape.

Her attire was pretty much the same as it always was – jeans, denim shirt and boots. She blended in perfectly.

Today they would be heading out to the boys' home in Enkosi and she would meet Jenna Pringle who had been running the place for the past year and a half. She would also be introduced to each of the boys. And, before the day was out, she would get Stone Hudson to kiss her.

Indie's lips curled at her private joke. Now where had that thought come from? She hadn't had that in her plans for the day. Not at all. But there it was. The thought had popped into her mind and now she couldn't get rid of it. Tessa's spontaneity and craziness was definitely rubbing off on her. And, as crazy as the idea was, she would do everything she could to make it happen. Time was going fast and she had to get this party started or she'd be on the losing end of this challenge. And Indiana Lane was not a loser.

The journey along the highway took a little over an hour until they turned off onto a smaller road that led into more rural terrain. Eventually the asphalt road ended and then they were bumping along a dirt road which became more like a track. That portion of the journey lasted almost forty-five minutes until finally they saw the compound up ahead. They pulled up in front of a long, low building painted white with a strip of red and yellow flowers running along the length of the wall. As the Jeep pulled up in the yard a very pregnant woman with fiery red hair ran out of the front door and headed toward them. Ran may not have been the best word choice, though. Waddled would be more accurate.

"Stone!" The woman didn't even wait for him to get out of the vehicle. As soon as she got close enough she reached into the open-back van and gave him a fierce hug.

As Indie watched she cocked an eyebrow. She couldn't help it. Strange employer-employee relationship, where the woman felt comfortable to hug her boss like that. But then again, she was pregnant. Indie would lighten up and give her that. When pregnant, anything was possible.

"I'm so glad you came back so soon," the woman was saying. "You would not imagine." Then she turned to look at Indie sitting in the back seat with her bags beside her. "And this is my salvation. Thank you so much for coming." And before Indie could even reply the woman had come around to the back seat, leaned over and was hugging her, too.

Indie couldn't do a thing but hug her back. She couldn't be rude, of course. And it seemed that the woman was a natural-born hugger.

The redhead pulled back then grinned at Indie. "I'm Jenna, by the way. Jenna Pringle. We're just finishing up lunch. Come on in and meet the boys."

She stepped back so that Indie could hop out of the Jeep and then she took her hand, leaving the men to follow them. There was no shyness about Jenna Pringle, not an ounce of reserve. She seemed to be the kind of person who would just welcome you into her home, no questions asked, no explanations expected. Was this how she'd be expected to behave in this job – effervescent and bubbly? If so, they'd have a long wait because Indie didn't do bubbly.

Jenna walked quickly but Indie's longer legs helped her keep up quite easily. Soon the three of them – the driver seemed to have disappeared – were in a long, brightly lit dining room with about ten tables around which sat boys ranging from toddlers to teenagers around fifteen or sixteen years old. As the visitors entered they all stood and, in unison, said a polite, "Good afternoon." They were smiling brightly and all eyes were on Stone. It was obvious to Indie that he was known and loved.

Jenna waved to them to be seated and as they did, the previously quiet dining room began to buzz with the chatter of sixty excited boys. One of the youngest, eyes bright as stars, jumped up from his seat and ran over to Stone where he wrapped his chubby arms around a green-clad leg.

"Mosola," Stone said with a smile and crouched down so his face was level with the child's. "Come give me a hug."

He got a huge smile and a hug around the neck that looked like it would cut off his air but he didn't seem to mind at all. Stone was laughing as he hugged him back then he stood up with the child still clinging to his neck. Soon another little one ventured forward then another, until Stone was surrounded by at least a dozen little boys, all demanding their hug. And Stone delivered.

Next, he went from table to table, greeting the older boys, addressing each of them by name. Indie wondered how he remembered them all but he seemed to have no trouble and it was clear that the boys appreciated the attention.

"He really loves those boys." It was Jenna, right by her elbow, and she was whispering to Indie. "And you'll love them, too, as soon as you get to know them. They're all so sweet. You'll see-"

She was cut off mid-sentence when a bell started to ring. "Lunch time is over," Jenna shouted over the din. "Time for the afternoon classes. Follow me."

The boys formed a neat line and without Jenna having to say a word they filed out of the dining room and off to wooden buildings that stood at various ends of the compound.

Jenna took Indie on a tour of the classrooms. "We have eleven teachers," she said, "covering the little ones in preschool right up to grade ten. For the higher grades the boys go on to high school in Johannesburg." They'd reached a building cheerfully painted yellow. She held the door open. "Welcome to your new home away from home. After today, she's all yours."

It was a neat little bungalow that seemed to serve as Jenna's office. A desk and file cabinet sat next to the sofa in the living room, partially hidden from view by a screen decorated with African print with stripes of orange, yellow and black. Surprisingly, the bedroom was the largest room in the house, with a huge four-poster bed with a canopy from which pale white curtains fell. A closer look told Indie those weren't curtains but mosquito netting. Smart move. She knew from personal experience how vicious the tiny insects could be.

"Make yourself comfortable." Jenna spread her arms wide. "The driver will soon bring your bags. The few things I have here are packed and ready to go. In fact," she lowered her voice in a conspiratorial whisper, "as soon as Stone called to say he was bringing you, my husband and I started clearing up the place. I was never so happy to lose a job." Then, as she saw Indie's face she laughed. "Oh, don't worry. It's one of the most rewarding jobs in the world. You'll love it. It's just that Kirk and I want to get ready for our baby. This will be our first and, being so busy, we haven't had a chance to prepare."

"When are you due?" As far as Indie was concerned that baby looked like it should have come out already. Jenna looked about ready to pop.

"In two weeks, but you know babies. They can come a couple of weeks early or a couple of weeks late. I could go into labor right now."

Indie put a hand on her arm. "Please. Don't. Let me at least get settled first."

The pregnant woman laughed and stroked her belly. "My baby has been good to me so far. I know she'll cooperate just a little bit longer."

"Oh, it's a girl? Have you chosen a name yet?"

"We're still working on that. We have some names on our list - Diamond, Crystal, Jessica. One of the teachers suggested Imani, which means faith."

"Very nice," Indie said, nodding. "I'm sure she'll be as beautiful as her name."

They were interrupted when there was a knock on the door and Jenna opened to see one of the teenage boys with a tray covered with a striped cloth. "Cook sent lunch for the lady," he said, and laid the tray in Jenna's arms.

"Thank you, Mfana." She took the tray and headed to the tiny dining room. "Come on, Indie," she said over her shoulder. "We can talk while you eat."

While Jenna brought her up to speed on what needed to be done to ensure the smooth operation of the home, Indie enjoyed a meal of boiled yams, curried chicken and carrot salad, also curried.

As she listened to Jenna talk, Indie realized that the job was going to be a lot more work than she'd thought. In addition to supervising the home with the assistance of six home mothers, Jenna was also principal of the school and she even filled in as substitute teacher when any of the staff members fell ill. Indie was going to have her hands full.

As long as she could find time to be with Stone.

She took a pause from her meal as she thought about that. Her primary purpose for being here was to get to know Stone – fast – and to get a marriage proposal, but based on all that Jenna had told her she didn't even know if she'd find time to go to the bathroom, let alone go man hunting. She grimaced. Things were not looking good.

"Don't worry, Indie. It's not that bad."

Indie blinked. She looked across the table at Jenna who was smiling at her.

"I know you're worried. I can see it on your face. But you'll be all right. The staff is very supportive. They're like my sisters and brothers." She reached over and patted Indie's arm. "And they'll give you all the help they gave me. I'm sure of it. They want this home to succeed just as much as we do."

Indie nodded. If Jenna only knew…

This was a good time to change the subject. "Where did Stone disappear to?"

"I guess he's spending time in each of the classrooms, chatting with the boys. He always does that. That's why they love him so much. We all do." She got up. "Now you finish eating. I'm going to get Kirk to pick up my stuff. "She left Indie and headed for the front door.

So this is it. Indie looked around. This little house would be her place of abode for the next few weeks, maybe a whole lot longer. She knew her personal weakness. Once she'd attached herself to a cause she would see it through to the end. And if she wasn't careful, whether things worked out with Stone or not, she'd most likely spend as long as it took to ensure

the success of the boys' home.

A few minutes later there was a rap at the front door and Indie opened to find a tall, gangly man with a shock of brown hair standing in the doorway.

"Hi," he said with a warm smile. "I'm Kirk, Jenna's husband. One of the drivers just dropped her home and she asked me to pass by."

"Yes, of course." Indie stepped aside. "Won't you come in?"

"Thanks." He brushed his palms against the seat of his very worn jeans. "Jenna said I should come over and pick up some bags. Do you know where they are?"

"I did see a couple of bags in the bedroom, in the corner by the window." She waved her hand toward the room. "Go on in. I'm sure those are the bags you're looking for."

He gave her a polite, almost apologetic nod, then headed for the bedroom. "Yep," he called out, "it's them all right. Jenna's forever tagging her bags with these little pink strips of cloth." He came out of the room with the bags tucked under his arms. "Ever since we heard it's a girl you would think pink is the only color in the world."

Indie gave him a sympathetic smile and went to hold the front door open. "She's just excited, that's all. As I'm sure you are, too."

His bashful smile and the blush creeping up his neck told Indie she was right. He gave her another quick nod and then he was through the door, lugging the bags toward an ancient-looking pickup truck. He threw them in the back then jumped into the cab. The engine turned over immediately, sounding like a very healthy, well-tuned machine, nothing like what the outside looked like. He gave her a wave. "If you need anything, just send one of the drivers to fetch me. I'm not even a quarter mile away."

"Will do." She waved until he disappeared down the dirt track.

Alone again, Indie headed back inside where she washed the lunch dishes then she sat down at the desk and began to go through the notes Jenna had left for her. Orders to be placed for school and home supplies, a staff meeting to be planned for the teachers two days from now, a progress report to do, one that Jenna hadn't even had the time to touch. Boredom would definitely not arise as one of her problems. Not at this place. There was just too much to do. Never one to procrastinate, Indie grabbed a notepad and began to write her plan of action.

She was absorbed in her second task, pulling the notes together for the progress report, when she heard a knock at the door. She looked up. How many hours had she been at it? She glanced over at the desk clock. Three-thirty in the afternoon already. Where had the past couple of hours gone? It seemed like less than half an hour since she'd sat down at the desk.

She got up and stretched then strode to the door. It was probably Kirk coming back for more of Jenna's stuff. She didn't mind. Although he seemed shy she might just strike up a conversation with him, maybe ask him a few things about the region.

She pulled the door open, a welcoming smile already on her face. But it wasn't Kirk who filled her doorway. It was Stone.

"Hey," he said, smiling down at her. "Overwhelmed yet?"

Indie laughed. "Not yet." Her heart feeling light with the pleasant surprise of his visit, she stepped back to let him in.

"Brave girl," he said as he ducked his head to step through the doorway. Then he turned to her. "But don't worry. You do have a second in command. A vice principal of sorts. Anita is her name. A competent woman. In fact, before Jenna came on board she held the fort for a good two months."

"That's good to know. I was wondering why Jenna departed so suddenly, like she was leaving me to sink or swim." Indie waved a hand, directing Stone over to the couch. "Good to know I have somebody here who knows the ropes."

"Of course." He sank into the chair and stretched his long legs out in front of him. "You need time to get your feet wet. Anita will pick up the slack while you're in learning mode. In fact," he crossed his ankles then rested an arm on the back of the chair, "you have a top class crew. All this ship needs is a good captain to keep her pointed in the right direction."

"I'm looking forward to it," she said, and she meant it. "I already have some ideas I'd like to implement in the home and even in the school." Warming to her subject, she sat in the armchair across from Stone and leaned forward. "What do you think about adding vocational subjects to the curriculum for the older boys? I remember in school I used to love tinkering with old cars. What if we offered introductory courses in auto mechanics, building construction and agriculture? The way I see it, it could only complement the academic curriculum. It certainly wouldn't hurt." She tilted her head. "What do you think?"

He shrugged. "I'm not an educator but from my layman's perspective I don't see why not. Why don't you lay out your proposal and I'll have someone from the ministry of education have a look at it? It might be worth getting the opinion of an expert."

"Consider it done," she said, relieved that he was taking her suggestion seriously. "It will be in your hands before this week is out."

"Sounds good to me. Anything that will prepare the boys for high school and for life, I'll support one hundred percent."

That made her pause and shake her head. "You're so dedicated to those boys. It's such a pleasure to find a wealthy man who cares enough to give to others."

That made him frown, but he looked more thoughtful than angry. "You find that strange? Most of my business associates have charities that they support wholeheartedly. Some of them give away millions every year."

Now it was Indie's turn to frown. "Really?"

Stone nodded. "Really." He pulled in his legs then sat forward and rested his elbows on his knees. "You know, rich people tend to get a bad rap but you'd be surprised at how many of them actually do a lot for the disadvantaged. The majority, I should guess."

Slowly, Indie nodded. "I think you may be right. All my adult life I've been dashing from country to country, working for various non-profit organizations, feeling good about myself for helping others. I never really gave enough thought to those people behind the scenes who may not have participated directly but were critical to the success of the projects through their financial contributions." She gave Stone a crooked smile. "I stand suitably chastised."

"You do, do you?" He gave her a suspiciously mischievous grin.

"I do."

"Well, I know one way you can make things up to us rich folks." She chuckled. "How?"

"You can have dinner with me tonight."

Had she heard right? "Did you just ask me out?" she demanded playfully.

"I did."

"So where are we going to have this dinner? At Café Out-in-the-Middle-of-Nowhere? We're practically in the wilderness."

"I'm inviting you to dinner at my house."

"At...your house." Now that was different and sort of...intriguing.

"It's just a cottage, really, no bigger than yours. Behind the main school building. My home away from home. So...are we on for dinner?"

Indie nodded. "I'd love to, just as long as you don't poison me with your cooking."

He laughed out loud. "Don't you worry about that. My meals come fully catered, complements of the home's resident chef."

"Oh." She pouted, feigning disappointment. "And there I was, thinking you were going to make a special effort just for me."

"Maybe next time." Stone got up and gave a leisurely stretch. "I'd better get going so I can tidy up before you come. So you'll be over around six?"

"Six is fine with me."

"Want me to come get you?"

"I'm sure I'll find it." Indie got up, too. "The compound is big but not that big that I can't find you."

"Great. I'll see you at six then."

He headed for the front door with Indie right behind him. As he let himself out she couldn't help but admire his broad shoulders. It must be because he was standing in the narrow doorway. It made him look big and strong, every bit the macho man.

He waved goodbye and as he walked away Indie stood in the doorway, staring after him, a soft smile on her face. Lady Luck was definitely on her side today. She couldn't have wanted a better turn of events.

CHAPTER SEVEN

Stone splashed water on his face and stared into the bathroom mirror. What was it about Indiana Lane that had him sweating like a damn teenager every time he was in her presence? For God's sake, he was a thirty-three year old man, way past the sweating and trembling stage. Was he regressing? That made him smile at his own reflection. That was a laugh. It must be the setting, all the way out here in this wilderness as Indie had called it. He couldn't remember reacting this strongly to a woman. Not since high school, anyway.

But now here he was, totally captivated by the woman with the emerald green eyes. And that was why, when he'd seen that opening, he hadn't been able to resist asking her over. At her place he'd acted nonchalant, like he'd already ordered dinner and everything was arranged. No such thing. He'd had to send a message to Cook real fast to fix a special dinner for two. Luckily, he already had wine chilling in the fridge.

He grabbed a towel and dried his face then headed for the living room. He hadn't been kidding when he said he needed to tidy up before Indie got there. He wasn't the neatest of souls and his mind immediately went to his mother. She'd been at him since he'd been able to understand the words 'pick up your clothes'. Where that was concerned, he was still a failure. *Sorry, Mom.*

At twenty minutes before six Cook's packages of food arrived. Stone slipped them into the oven to keep them warm then he went and got dressed in dark slacks and a creamy silk shirt. At three minutes before the hour of six there was another knock at the door and the long-awaited lady stood there looking elegant in gray slacks and a peach-colored top that showed off her bare shoulders.

"Welcome." He held the door open for her and as she stepped past, her perfume brought back memories of that first night they'd dined together. That night she'd looked exquisite, like a perfectly painted porcelain doll. Tonight was different. Tonight she looked relaxed, natural and so inviting. He wanted to bend down and press his lips to the smooth skin of her shoulder then to her collarbone, her neck, then her lips.

He began to grow hard again and he had to step back and take a deep breath. What was with him tonight? Just the sight of her, her fragrance, had him thinking crazy thoughts. She fit so well into this earthy, untamed setting that his thoughts ran to things hot and wild – like her, straddling his hips and making mad love to him.

Stone shook his head. If he didn't slow down he was going to get himself in a whole lot of trouble.

"So," he said, shoving his hands deep into his pockets, "welcome to my home."

"You already said that." She gave him a look of amusement then her eyes scanned the room. "You were right. It looks just like my place."

He spread his arms wide. "See? We're all equals in this place. No need to bash the rich guy."

"I wasn't going to." She cocked an eyebrow at him. "Not unless he gives me reason to."

"I won't." He put his hands up and backed away. "Trust me, I know when I'm in the presence of a warrior woman."

He'd meant that as a joke but at his words she looked a little hurt. "I mean, you look like you can defend yourself," he said quickly, trying to do damage control.

"It's okay," she said, her voice punctuated with a sigh. "Part of the territory, being taller than most other women. People see you as a whole lot tougher than you actually are."

"I didn't mean that-"

"It's okay," she said again, her voice insistent. "Let's just eat."

That shut Stone up for a while. This was something she was obviously sensitive about and pressing her further would only make things worse. As much as he found every inch of her to be a tantalizing treat now was not the time to tell her that. She would think he was just trying to make her feel better. *Great going, Stone, you just put your size twelve foot in it.* Wanting to melt her frosty mood, Stone turned on the CD player and the sounds of Shania Twain's 'From This Moment' filled the room. The soothing sounds should calm her down. As he went to pull out her chair he saw that her mouth was just a little less tight and the furrow between her brows gone. Whew.

He lifted the white wine from its bed of ice and poured her a glass. Then he got the meal from the oven – salmon in a light lemon sauce with wild rice and a vegetable medley. Indie's eyes widened at the sight of the elegantly prepared trays. "Cook did this?"

"Yep. A man of many talents. He can serve the Queen of England, if called on."

Indie nodded. "I have no doubt."

After that, it was as if that awkward moment had never happened. They fell into easy conversation, with Indie plying him with questions about his family back in Canada. He told her about his older sister who lived in Vancouver and was a professor of

Medieval History at the university there, and his younger brother, also a businessman, who had moved to Australia with his young wife and infant son. And then there were his mom and dad, stalwarts in the Toronto community, members of the Chamber of Commerce and philanthropists in their own right.

"The Hudson wing at the Toronto City Hospital is named after them."

"So that's where you get it from, this philanthropy thing."

He shrugged. "I do my own thing."

"Yes, you do," she said, her voice a sultry whisper that made Stone wonder if they were still talking about philanthropy. Somehow, it didn't sound like it.

Indie had leaned forward, her elbows on the table, her hands folded in front of her, her chin resting on those folded hands. And she was looking at him with half closed eyes, her lips slightly parted.

And if she kept that up she was going to get a whole lot more than dinner tonight.

Stone clenched and unclenched his hands under the table. If Indie only knew what he wanted to do right now. Then again, maybe she already did, and that was why she was playing temptress tonight. And he wanted to make a move, no doubt about that. But he had to be sure.

"All right," Stone said, picking up his napkin and giving a last swipe at his lips, "looks like we're done here." He got up and held out his hand to Indie. "Why don't we head to the living room? There's something I want to show you."

"Oh. All right." Indie took his hand and rose to stand beside him.

It took a whole lot of willpower for him not to drag her into his arms and kiss her breathless. But no, now was not the time.

Stone led Indie to the small sofa in the living room then crouched down in front of the VCR on the TV stand.

"Old movies," Indie guessed.

"Yes, but not just any old movies. My old movies." Stone slid the first tape in, pressed play then went to sit at the other end of the couch. "These are recordings of my earlier trips to South Africa. I made a lot of cultural mistakes and maybe you can learn from some of them. And I had a lot of fun."

They settled back in the chair and watched shots of Stone arriving in South Africa, meeting with government officials, then his first meeting with Moekebi. The child was thin but with eyes so bright and full of life you couldn't help but be buoyed up by his spirit. Then there was the opening of the boys' home and the installation of the teachers. And, to Stone's horror, there was also a clipping of him in native dress doing a traditional dance. He'd forgotten about that.

Indie howled with laughter at that one. "Oh, my Lord, what were you thinking?" She was laughing so much tears filled her eyes. "No, that was not the act of Stone Hudson. That had to be Gladstone doing that dance. There's no way a 'Stone' would be doing that. You can't even dance!" And with that she burst into peels of laughter again.

"You'd better take that back," he growled. "Or else."

"Or else what?" Her mouth curled in amusement and defiance.

"Or else you'll be punished," he said, moving closer.

"Yeah? How?" she challenged, her eyes flashing in the light.

"Like this," he said with a groan, then he was reaching for her, unable to deny himself any longer. He dragged Indie off the sofa and onto his lap and then he dipped his head and was kissing her with all the desire he'd been holding back for so long. As his arms circled her, pulling her close, his mouth held hers captive, demanding her response, and when she gave it, kissing him back with a fervor matching his own, he moaned.

When Stone finally lifted his head and looked into Indie's eyes they were no longer sharp but had turned misty-green with passion. She sighed and leaned against him, soft and pliable in his arms.

It was too much. He lowered his head and kissed her again, this time more softly, more sweetly, more deeply, until she was clinging to him.

"Stone," Indie whispered, "I've wanted this for so long."

Stone's heart swelled inside him. Indie wanted him. Could it be possible that she wanted him as badly as he wanted her? He could only hope. But her whisper was enough to give him that hope.

"Oh God, Indie," he groaned. "I want you...too much. But I've got to stop now or else..." He didn't say the rest. He knew exactly where this would end if he didn't regain control. Stone slid Indie off his lap and back onto the sofa. Then he got up and shoved his hands into his pockets. As he looked down at her he shook his head.

"It's okay," she said with a small smile. "I understand." She got up and reached out to touch his arm. "Walk me to the door?"

He stared down at her, his eyes burning into hers. "See you tomorrow?

She lifted her eyebrows. "We'll see."

"Have dinner with me again." He'd said that on an impulse, but he meant it.

"I'll do better than that," she said. "Tomorrow I'll fix dinner for you."

That took him by surprise. Things could not have worked out better. "I'll be there at six."

She went on tiptoe and kissed him on the cheek then she whispered in his ear, "I look forward to it."

. . ⧉ . .

TWENTY-FOUR DAYS TO the deadline and things were heading in the right direction. And the surprise was, she hadn't even been the one to send them down that road.

Just like she'd planned, he'd kissed her. Because he wanted to. She hadn't had a thing to do with it. Well, almost nothing.

She had to admit that she might have had just a tiny bit of influence on him. She'd worn that perfume she knew he'd fallen in love with that first night they'd had dinner together. She'd seen his reaction when he breathed in the fragrance. And then she'd worn her killer blouse, the one that revealed a whole lot of shoulder and just a hint of cleavage. And, to top it all off, she'd given him the 'eye' just like Tessa had taught her, keeping her eyes half closed and setting her lips in an inviting pout.

And then he'd kissed her, so her preening must have worked. Or he must have really, really liked her. She liked reason number two better.

The fact was, she wanted him to like her. For real. Because, for her, all of this was growing a lot more serious than just like. She was beginning to fall in love.

It was strange. Could a woman fall in love in the space of six days? According to the Psychology books she'd read it was men who would usually say they'd fallen in love at first sight. Women spent more time in getting to know the man before admitting to such feelings.

But, from that first meeting, she'd felt that connection. It was freaky but the mere sight of him had set her body blazing. Had he felt the same way? Was that the real reason he'd kissed her last night?

She drew in a deep breath, the thoughts bumping around in her head, and stared out her bedroom window at the sun rising over the plains. With all she had to do, today was going to be hectic. And she would have to fix dinner for Stone. Well, actually, she planned to ask Cook to do it. Cooking was not exactly one of her best skills. Fishing? Yes. Maybe even catching some wild game, like birds or rabbits. But cooking? Please.

She pulled the mosquito netting aside and slid out of bed. She might as well get started early. She was looking forward to a productive day and, if all went well, a very exciting evening.

Anita came to get Indie just after eight o'clock so she got a chance to have breakfast with the boys. Then after they'd filed away to their classes she toured each room and got to know them individually. The little ones were really excited to have her, and climbed onto her lap and pulled her hair which was growing a little longer. They wouldn't let her leave until she'd read them a story and then another until finally, hugging them and laughing at their antics, she was able to slip out.

She toured the other classes and was able to note their needs. Later she would write a requisition list. After that it was time to examine the housing facilities and determine what needed to be done. By the time she'd done her tours it was almost three in the afternoon, she'd missed lunch, and she hadn't even had time to speak to Cook yet.

Of course, when she did speak to him he was none too pleased at the short notice and he held nothing back in telling her so. Still, after much cajoling and wheedling, she got him to agree to prepare a simple meal of chicken stew with mashed potatoes and sweet corn.

That settled, she hurried back to her cottage-cum-office where she did paperwork until about five o'clock. At that point she had to break to get herself ready for her dinner date. She was pleasantly surprised when the meal arrived at five-twenty, long before she'd even had a chance to dress and fix her hair. Not that there was much to fix, it was so short. But still, she wanted to look her best.

This evening she softened her look, forgoing the slacks for a flowing, ankle-length dress with a slit that ran up her left calf and halfway up her thigh. She knew she had nice legs. She'd received her fair share of compliments. And tonight she planned to give Stone a peek so he could see what he was missing.

And that idea was all her own. No Tessa, no Cosmopolitan Magazine, all Indie.

She set the table and, on an impulse, she set a short, fat scented candle in the middle and lit it. She'd found the candle in one of the kitchen cupboards and why should she let it go to waste? More importantly, she was trying to draw this man in so she might as well go all the way.

As the sun began to slide toward the horizon Indie went to the door and looked out. And there, striding toward her house, tall and dark with the setting sun to his back, was Stone.

At the sight of him her heart gave a flutter. Sure, she was expecting him and, of course, this wasn't their first dinner date. But still, she couldn't stop her heart from jerking in anticipation. Involuntarily she pulled at her dress, letting it fall softly around her legs, then she reached up a hand and smoothed her hair back and away from her face. The fluttery feeling in the pit of her stomach told her she was nervous as hell. *Come on, Indie, you've done this before. Just chill out.*

Stone was at her door now, and as he stepped forward she tilted her chin up, her face deliberately cool and serene, and accepted his peck on the cheek. He would never guess that her placid exterior was just a sham. Inside she was as jumpy as quicksilver.

"Now it's my turn to welcome you," she said with a soft smile as he stepped inside.

He didn't reply but the intensity of his gaze was all the response she needed. He was taking her in, all of her, from the top of her head down to her sandaled feet peeping out from under the hem of her dress. And his eyes lingered in all the right places – the sweep of her collarbone, the slope of her neckline and all the way up that all-important slit in the side of her dress.

His glance slid back to her face and when he realized that she'd been following his eyes he straightened his back and cleared his throat. A hint of a flush told her he was embarrassed at being caught.

But she didn't mind the attention at all. She welcomed it. It was a very encouraging sign.

"Make yourself comfortable." She gave him a reassuring smile. "You must be thirsty after your walk. I'll get you a drink."

When she got to the kitchen she drew in a deep breath then let it out slowly. Staying in control was not going to be as easy as she'd thought. Having him so close – the woodsy fragrance of his cologne, the fact that he was sitting right there in her living room – was sending her pulse racing like she'd just done a five mile run.

Even her fingers were shaking. Yikes! She really had to get a hold of herself or he'd think she'd gone batty.

She let a few seconds pass and then, pasting a smile on her face, she exited the kitchen carrying the two chilled glasses of wine. She was surprised when she saw that Stone had found the chess game that had been sitting on top of the bookcase. He'd opened the box and was laying out the pieces as she entered the room.

"You like chess," she said matter-of-factly. It was not a question. He just looked like a man who would be good at that sort of game.

He shrugged and continued to place the pieces. "I'm competitive. What can I say?" Then he looked up at her and grinned. "Want to play?"

She gave him a crooked smile. "I don't know..." He looked like he could give her a good whipping and she didn't know if she wanted to lose to him tonight. Maybe some other time but tonight she wanted to be a winner in every sense of the word. She handed him his glass of wine and went over to sit on the seat across from him then she slid back in the chair, relaxed, and took a sip.

"Chicken?" He gave her a cheeky grin.

"Never." But still, she didn't move closer to the board. "I'll take you up on your challenge," she said, "after dinner." With any luck after dinner they'd be too occupied to even remember about a chess game.

Stone seemed unperturbed. He shrugged his broad shoulders and lounged in the sofa, watching her over the rim of his glass as he sipped. With his brown eyes near golden and the dark-brown hair framing his rugged face he could have been a lion basking in the warmth of the South African sun, casually regarding his prey. But she was the hunter, not the hunted. She didn't like feeling like prey.

"Let's head for the dining room before our food gets cold," she said and stood up so he would, too. He complied and followed her out of the living room.

When Stone saw the romantic setting, the meal laid out, the tiny vase with bright orange daisies in the middle of the table and the stout red candle beside it, he whistled.

That brought a blush to Indie's cheeks. Had she been too presumptuous to make this look like a real date? The man was her employer, after all.

But no, he was looking at the table then at her with nothing but appreciation.

She relaxed then, and they sat down to a meal punctuated with laughter and ribbing until Indie couldn't even remember what she'd been uptight about.

After that they moved to the living room where Indie was able to convince Stone to try Monopoly instead of chess. With that game choice, she thought, she would have some hope of winning. No such luck. Stone whipped her three times in a row till she threatened to confiscate the board and send him packing.

He only laughed. "Now it's time for you to pay," he growled and moved closer to her on the sofa.

"Pay?" Her brows shot up and her eyes widened. "I didn't know there was a penalty for losing."

"There is," he said, his tone unapologetic.

"Since when?" She gave him her sternest look. She was not used to being bullied, especially not by a man.

"Since now," he said, his voice a sexy whisper.

Indie's breath caught in her throat. Stone Hudson was trying to seduce...her.

She had no time to dwell on that thought. He was reaching for her and her body, eager as it was for his touch, was leaning toward him, betraying the depth of her desire. And then she was in his arms, her breasts crushed against his rock-hard chest, her lips pressed against his.

Stone kissed her urgently, plundering her mouth, wiping from her mind everything but the feel of him, the taste of him, the scent of his cologne.

And as urgent as he was kissing her she was kissing back. Indie wrapped her arms around Stone's waist and held on as they rode the waves of passion together.

When Stone released her lips he was breathing hard. "I want you, Indie," he said in a ragged whisper. "I want you so bad."

He reached for her again and just like last time he dragged her onto his lap but this time his lips skimmed past hers and slid down the length of her neck to her collarbone and then to that sensitive valley between her breasts where his hot breath tickled and tantalized till she arched up to meet his mouth.

Yes, he wanted her. She could hear it in the heavy thumping in his chest, see it in the perspiration that beaded his brow and feel it in the hardness that pressed up into her thigh.

And she wanted him. And when his lips slid even lower to kiss the top of her right breast, she reached up to pull his head down, urging him on, wanting more.

When Stone slid his lips lower and captured her nipple, Indie gasped.

A jolt ran through her body and then she was melting inside as pure pleasure flowed from his lips. She sank against him, her body weak and pliable in his arms. And when his hand slid down to the slit in her dress and slowly ran up the length of her thigh she could only moan at his sweet seduction.

Indie was floating on air when Stone lifted his head then slid his arm behind her knees. He got up from the sofa and, in one smooth move, he had lifted her into his arms and was striding out of the room.

"What?" Confused, Indie clung to his shoulders but when she looked up into his face what she saw left her in no doubt as to his intentions.

In just a few purposeful strides Stone was in her bedroom and then he was laying her gently on the bed. He lay down beside her and his golden-brown eyes flashed as he gazed down at her. "You know what I want, Indie," he said, his voice hoarse, "but do you want this, too?"

"I..." She swallowed. What should she say? The question wasn't if she wanted him – there was no doubt in her mind about that – but would he want her? How would he react when she told him she was, at almost the grand old age of thirty, still a virgin?

"I..." She tried again, but no words came. For a woman who was used to being in control it was as if she'd lost the power of speech. The sad thing was, when it came to sex she was out of her depth.

"It's okay," Stone whispered. "If you're not ready I can wait. I want this to be your decision."

A wave of embarrassment washed over Indie. She ducked her face and pressed it against his shoulder. Oh God, this was awful. Should she tell him and risk being laughed at or should she remain silent and leave him thinking she was being a tease?

She gritted her teeth and reached out to cling to him. Then she drew in a deep breath and took the plunge. "I've never done this before. This would be my...first time."

Stone went still. Even his breathing stopped. Then he reached up and loosened her fingers which still clutched his shoulders. He pulled back and looked into her face. "Your first time?"

She dropped her gaze, her heart aching at the incredulity she'd seen on his face. She nodded then waited for the anger. Or the ridicule.

But none came. Instead, she was shocked when he pulled her into his arms and gave her a sweet, gentle kiss on the forehead. "Thank you," he said softly as he held her close.

Indie frowned. Of all the things he could have said she was not expecting a thank you. She pulled back and peered up at him. "For what?"

He reached up a hand to stroke the strands of disheveled hair away from her face. "Thank you for telling me." He smiled. "Your first time...it has to be special. And it will be, but not tonight. I will wait till the time is right."

At his words Indie closed her eyes and laid her head on his chest. She'd waited so long to share that special moment with the man of her heart. Now that she'd found him how much longer would she wait? When the time was right, he'd said. She prayed it would be sometime soon.

CHAPTER EIGHT

It was now nineteen days to Indie's deadline and although her relationship with Stone had progressed, with him checking up on her at least twice a day, she was still nervous. A lot could happen in nineteen days. And on the other hand, nothing could happen. Had she come this far only to fail?

But who was she kidding? Where on God's green earth did two people meet, fall in love, and get married in thirty days? Not counting Las Vegas. Maybe she should have gone to Vegas to do her manhunt.

But seriously, was this a lost cause? She looked again at the calendar on the wall, at the big red X's marking off the days, and she heaved a sigh. Somehow she had to find a way to speed things up...without Stone noticing, of course.

Ever since he'd found out she was a virgin he'd backed off. It wasn't that he was ignoring her. He came by the school every day and greeted her with a warmth she should have no complaints about. Except that it wasn't warmth that she wanted. It was passion, craving and even...love. But was she destined to ever find that elusive prize, particularly within the next two and a half weeks?

She set her lips in a determined pout and got up from behind the desk. If anything was going to happen she would have to make it happen. She'd always believed in creating her own destiny and she wasn't going to stop now. She marched out of the cottage, intent on finding Stone. She had no idea what she would do when she saw him but whatever it was, it was going to take her a whole lot closer to getting married than where she was now.

But when she went to Stone's cottage he was nowhere to be found. She went in search of Jenna.

"I'm sorry, Indie. He was called suddenly to the HBC office in Johannesburg. He wanted to tell you before leaving but you weren't in your office or at the school." Jenna gave her an apologetic look. "He asked me to tell you but I was swamped this morning. I didn't get a chance to come find you."

"No, that's okay," Indie said, her thoughts scattered. "I understand. I know you're busy getting ready for the baby." She bit her lip. She would just have to be patient. Stone would be back soon enough. Johannesburg was only two and a half hour's drive away. She turned back to Jenna. "Did he say what time he'd be back?"

"He said he'd be gone three, maybe four days."

Three or four days. In Indie's world that was a lifetime. She was already down to the wire and then to lose that many days? Her heart sank. So near to her goal and yet so far. There was nothing she could do but wait.

But Indie did not have to wait long before excitement hit the compound. The following day she was in the classroom with the ninth graders when Kirk rushed up to the door.

"My truck won't start. Where's the driver?" He was breathing hard as if he'd run all the way from his house.

"Fenyang is away on holiday. He went back to his township but Dominic should be around here somewhere." Then, seeing desperation leap into his eyes, Indie got up from her chair and hurried to him. "What's wrong? Is it Jenna?"

"Yes, and the truck won't start and...and...I just have to find the driver." Kirk looked just about ready to pull out his hair.

"Boys," Indie yelled over her shoulder, "I'll be right back." She grabbed Kirk's arm. "Come on. I'll find Dominic. You go back and stay with Jenna. Don't leave her alone."

Kirk ran off across the yard and Indie headed straight for the kitchen. There were not that many places on the compound where a young man could hang out and the kitchen was a likely place to start.

And there he was, resting in the back while Cook and his assistants chopped carrots on the counter.

As soon as Indie explained the situation Dominic dashed off to get his Jeep and then he was off to Kirk and Jenna's place. Minutes later the van roared through the gate of the compound to the cheers of the ninth grade boys who had sneaked out of their classroom.

After that exciting turn of events nothing happened. Three days passed and Stone did not return. Then it was four days and then five. Meanwhile, the clock kept ticking toward her deadline.

Six days into the wait Indie heard the roar of the Jeep and it was Stone, finally back from his mission in Johannesburg. He'd called a couple of times during his absence but how could a phone call from over a hundred miles away help her?

And then, when she went out into the yard and saw him striding toward her, she knew that it hadn't just been about the marriage. It had been about Stone. She'd missed him terribly and now, at the sight of him, she wanted to run into his arms.

But she couldn't. Instead, she waited until he was standing right in front of her. She looked up and to her relief she could see in his eyes that he'd missed her, too.

That look in his eyes spoke volumes. It was a look well worth the wait.

· · ❧ · ·

IT WAS THREE DAYS LATER when they got the call. Jenna had delivered a seven-pound baby girl.

Indie could only laugh when she heard the news. "Can you imagine, they tore out of here a week ago, all because of a false labor. But I'm glad they didn't come back. Joburg was the safest place for Jenna to be."

"Particularly since she needed a C-section," Stone said, then he tilted his head toward Indie. "What do you think about you and me going to the city to meet this new member of the family?"

"I think that's the best thing you've said to me since you got back." Indie knew she probably looked like an idiot with the wide grin on her face but she didn't really care. She was dying to get off the compound, and she wanted to see the new baby. And to take a trip to Johannesburg with Stone – what better way to spend some alone time with him? "When can we leave? Now?"

He shook his head. "First thing in the morning. We can set out at sunrise and have the whole day ahead of us."

She frowned. She would lose a whole day waiting for tomorrow to come. "What about this afternoon? After lunch?"

He looked doubtful. "None of the drivers can take us this afternoon. I would have to drive us in that case."

Even better. No driver to get in the way of their conversation.

"No problem, though," he continued. "I've traveled that route so many times I know it like the back of my hand."

She chuckled. "You'd need to have a very big hand to cover that terrain. Just make sure you travel with a map. Better yet, get Cook to draw you one. I know there are some sections probably not on a regular map."

He shook his head. "So little faith in me," he tut-tutted.

Indie rolled her eyes. "Just get the map."

They ended up leaving the compound at a little past four o'clock. She had underestimated the time it would take to pack and be ready. Still, although they were heading out over an hour later than planned, for a journey of two and a half hours they'd be in Johannesburg by the set of sun.

Stone threw the bags into the back of the vehicle and Indie hopped into the passenger seat beside him. He looked over at her. "Ready to roll?"

She put her hand to her brow, and gave him a smart salute. "Aye, aye, Cap'n."

They set off along the dirt trail, leaving a cloud of dust behind them. Indie relaxed into the seat, a smile on her lips. She and Stone would get a chance to talk along the way and maybe she would be able to convince him to spend a few days in Johannesburg.

She'd already lost so much time she was hoping that a change in environment, a return to city life, would be the catalyst that would push Stone over the edge toward a commitment. Indie sighed. It was going to be hard, if not impossible. How do you get a man to ask you to marry him...without asking him to marry you?

Stone glanced over at her. "You all right?"

"Yes," she said, giving him a bright smile. "Perfect."

But she was far from it. Now back to her musings – how to get a man to ask you to marry him? Outside of hypnotizing him or blackmailing him, that is. Or maybe she could just knock him out and get a minister to marry them while he was still out cold. She was almost muttering in her distress. *Come on, brain, think. There's got to be something I can do.*

Indie bit her lip and looked away over the wide expanse of brown savannah. Stone was glancing over at her again. He must think she was going bananas. And rightly so. She was certainly acting like it.

Trying for normalcy, she decided to strike up a conversation. "Do you know if they picked out a name yet?" She put up a hand to keep her hat from hopping off her head. Stone had better get to a smooth path soon or she'd be seasick.

"I have no idea." He looked totally unconcerned.

"Hey, what if we come up with some suggestions? Wouldn't it be great if they liked one of our names and used it?" She was half speaking half shouting so he could hear her over the rumble of the engine.

Stone looked at her like she'd gone crazy. "What do I know about baby girl names?"

"Well, I have some. What about...Sierra? Or..." she looked around at the flat grass land, "...Savannah?"

He snorted, seeming unimpressed.

She didn't let that stop her from thinking up some more. "Hey, I got one. What about Safari?"

He glanced over at her again but this time he was shaking his head and his look was full of pity.

"No," she said earnestly, "I'm serious. It's a Swahili word that means long journey. And they journeyed all the way here to work at the compound, didn't they?" She looked away. "Safari," she said again, almost to herself. "I like it. I'm going to suggest it to them."

"Please don't," he groaned as he steered the vehicle over the dirt path.

"Please, yes," she said. "They'll love it."

After that they got to talking about her name and how she came about having it. Indiana, she explained, was for the state in which she was born. Although born of Canadian parents her birth certificate showed that she was an American citizen.

Moon, she told him, was for the time of year she was born, when the moon was full in the sky. And Lane was her absentee father's name.

"Moon," Stone repeated. "Somehow I thought it was a reflection of Native American heritage."

"Well, I'm part Mohawk on my mother's side," she said, "so you sort of guessed right."

He grinned at her, obviously pleased with himself.

Indie grinned back. *Oh, don't be too pleased with yourself, fella. I'm not done with you yet.* "And what about your name?" she asked. "How did you come to be called Gladstone Hudson? And do you have a middle name, by the way?"

That wiped the smile off his face real fast. His brows lowered and his mouth set in a hard line.

Indie burst out laughing. "If you could see your face. You look like a three year old who's just been told he has to go to bed."

That made Stone cough and then he chuckled and then he was laughing out loud just like she was. The wide open savannah echoed with the sounds of their mirth.

After the laughter died and she'd caught her breath Indie wiped her eyes and looked at Stone. "Seriously, though, who gave you that name? Your mom?"

Stone gave an exaggerated sigh and shook his head. "Gladstone Marcus Hudson the third. It was my grandfather's name then my father's and now it's mine. The curse of the Gladstones."

She gave him a look of sympathy. "Please don't inflict that kind of punishment on your son."

He chuckled. "The suffering ends here."

After that they fell silent for a while and Indie sat back to enjoy the landscape and the view of brown mountains in the distance. Then she closed her eyes to enjoy the warmth of the evening sun. After a long while she yawned and opened her eyes again. Better to stay awake and keep Stone's company. She glanced over and noticed that he was frowning. Then he began to mutter under his breath.

She sat up immediately. "Is something wrong?'

For a while he didn't answer but just kept scowling and muttering until she knew something was definitely wrong. "Talk to me, Stone. What is it?"

His scowl deepened then he gave a quick shake of his head as if annoyed. "I'm not...seeing the landmarks I should be seeing by now. There's supposed to be a rock-"

"Are we lost? Are you telling me you don't know where we are?" Indie gripped the top of the passenger door. This was not good.

"Not lost, just...on the wrong track, somehow." Stone did not look at her, just kept his eyes on the trail ahead.

Indie frowned. "Come to think of it, we should have hit the main road by now. We've been on this road over an hour." She looked around. "And didn't we pass that butte like half an hour ago?"

Stone didn't answer but the muttering started again.

Indie jerked forward. "Let's check the map. That should help us figure out where we are." When Stone made no move to hand it to her she spoke louder. "The map, Stone. In fact, both of them. Let me look at them while you drive."

Still no answer.

That made her suspicious. Then she spoke again and her voice was calm and steady as if she had no concern in the world. "You don't have the maps, do you?"

He shook his head as if to get rid of some annoying gnats and kept his eyes on the road.

"Do you, Stone?"

"No, I don't, all right?" His voice was an angry bark. "I didn't think I'd need them."

"You didn't think..." Her voice trailed off as she stared across at him. Then she continued with a scathing rebuke. "The operative words being, 'I didn't think'. What the hell were you thinking?"

"Just be quiet, will you?" Came his biting retort. "I need to concentrate."

"You need to concentrate," Indiana muttered. "Concentrate on getting us lost is what you're doing. No map. And now we're lost all the way out in this wild countryside." He shot her an angry look and she shut up. Pissing him off was not going to work. Better to spend her energy thinking of a way to get them out of this mess. She did a quick calming exercise, breathing in and breathing out three times and only then did she speak again. "How long ago did you realize you weren't on the right track?"

There was a delay of about ten seconds then Stone responded. "About twenty minutes ago."

"About twenty min-" Indie stared at him in disbelief. "But you didn't say anything."

"I thought I'd just drive some more, see if a familiar landmark showed up."

Indie wanted so badly to blast him but she held her tongue. He was a man, after all. He couldn't help it. For some reason unknown to humankind men could never be influenced to ask for directions. Or, in this case, to get a damn map. *Okay, Indie, stay calm. Blowing your top is not going to help anybody.*

She looked ahead at the sun sliding toward the horizon. "Okay, we have about forty to fifty minutes of daylight left. How are we on gas?"

"Good," he said, visibly relaxing now that she'd changed her tone. "A little over half a tank."

"Okay." She raised herself up and leaned over to where her backpack lay on the back seat. She dug around till she found her notebook then pulled a pen from the outside pocket. She looked around ,surveying the terrain, then began to sketch. "Immediately you had a doubt you should have said something to me," she said, not looking up. "There's no shame in asking for help."

"Yeah, yeah," Stone said, his tone sarcastic. "Ask for help from a girl. Everyone knows that women have no sense of direction."

"What? Don't let me slap you upside your head. And I would do it, too, if we weren't in such a dangerous position. We're on the African continent, in case you'd forgotten. The land of lions and hyenas." She glanced to the back of the Jeep. "Speaking of which, does this Jeep have a cover?"

He glanced at her then focused again on the road.

Oh Lord, that obviously meant no. They were in big trouble. She rose up again and reached over to slide her hand into her backpack. She pulled out a curved dagger with jagged edges. It was almost a foot long.

Stone glanced over at her and did a double take. "What the hell? Where did you get that?"

"My backpack," she said, her tone casual. "You didn't think I was coming all the way to Africa without protection, did you?"

He still looked stunned. "But...do you even know how to use that thing?"

She slid her thumb along the thin edge of the blade, testing its sharpness. "Who? Sylvester? He's served me well over the years. Skinned many a rabbit, gutted lots of fish. Great at peeling the hide from a deer."

His eyes widened as he stared at her. "You're a hunter?"

She grinned. "Let's put it this way. I hunt a lot better than I cook." She slid the big knife beneath her thigh and picked up her paper again. "The sun sets in the west so Johannesburg is that way as the crow flies." She pointed in the direction exactly opposite to where Stone was heading. "You need to turn around and head back the way you came."

He gave her a doubtful look. "Are you sure?"

"Positive." She didn't take her eyes off him until he began to turn the Jeep around. "Tell me something," she said, "are you carrying a weapon?"

He glared at her as if she shouldn't have had to ask. "Shotgun. It's on the floor in the back."

She gave him a brusque nod. "Good. If any animals decide to come sniffing around we can scare them off with that." She gave a snort. "God help us if a whole pride of lions decides to take us on."

He was looking over at her again, seeming bemused. "Aren't you scared?"

"More than I've ever been in my life."

"You don't look it," he said, lifting an eyebrow.

"Yeah, well I'm good at hiding my emotions."

"You can say that again."

After that they fell silent, he concentrating on the trail and she watching for signs of animals in the distance. "Do you have any binoculars?" she asked.

"Dashboard."

She reached over and pulled it out and immediately began perusing the brush and trees in the distance. "It's going to get dark soon," she said, her voice low, "and I want to know what I'm up against when the sun goes down."

He didn't say anything for a while then he blew out his breath. "See anything?"

"Nope. But that doesn't mean they aren't out there." She dropped the binoculars. "Pull over for a sec. I want to check something."

"I don't know about that, Indie. Right now I'd say let's not stop anywhere unless we have to. Animals are more likely to stay away from a moving vehicle than a stationary one.

"No, stop," she said again, her voice brooking no dissent.

He stopped.

Indie hopped out of the Jeep then walked off the trail and to a patch of dirt surrounded by clumps of grass. She dropped to her knees and peered at the markings in the dirt. Then she got up and followed a faint trail of dirt across the grass. She stopped after just a few yards and stared out over the flatland toward the copse of straggly trees.

When she got back to the Jeep Stone was frowning at her. "Any signs of animals?"

"Yep, and it's not good news." She climbed into the Jeep and slammed the door shut. "No lion but a cheetah was here recently. Can't be too far away." She gave him a serious look. "And cheetahs run damn fast."

"Okay," he said pressing on the gas, "let's get out of here."

"Not without a plan."

"Which is?"

She glanced at the gas gauge. "Based on my estimate on how far we are from our destination we have just enough gas to get us there. As long as we don't get lost again. So..." she stood up in the vehicle and when the wind blew off her hat she didn't even look back, "...I'll navigate while you drive. That way we won't waste any gas driving around in circles."

She heard a grumble at that but he didn't say anything out loud. He'd better not. At this stage she was their only hope of not spending the night keeping company with the wildlife of Africa.

"Now step on it, Hudson," she yelled. "Let's eat up some miles before the sun turns in for the night."

They drove fast but they drove carefully, with Indie stopping Stone a few times along the way so she could check the trail and keep their nose pointed in the right direction. Night was fast approaching and Indie kept watching the sun slipping closer and closer to the horizon. *Come on, sun. Stay with us a while longer. Just till we find the road.*

She was trying not to show it but she had a sinking feeling they weren't going to make it to civilization tonight. It was already dusk and the shadows of night were beginning to shroud the savannah. And if they ended up spending the night in the wild she wasn't sure an army knife and a shotgun would be any guarantee that they'd get out alive.

She was just about to stop Stone one more time when he gave a shout. "I see it. That's the landmark I was looking for."

Indie peered straight ahead. She didn't see a thing she would call a landmark. "What is it?" she yelled.

"That rock with the little chip at the side. See? It's an arrow pointing north." He grinned at her excitedly then he was laughing out loud as the Jeep roared toward the rock.

"That?" Indie said, incredulous. "That little rock is your landmark? No wonder you missed it."

"Well, I was right and we can't get lost after this," he yelled back. "I know exactly where I'm going."

Oh Lord, not again. Indie rolled her eyes. "Are you sure, Stone? Don't you think we should head back to the compound?"

"No way. From here we're closer to Joburg. Better to keep going." He laughed again. "Don't you worry your pretty little head. I'll get you there safe and sound."

Indie rolled her eyes again. "I give up," she said and flopped back down into the seat. Now that Stone had found his way he was all macho man again. She didn't have the heart to remind him that she was the one who had taken them back to their route. "Wake me when we get there," she said in a grumpy growl as she tried to block out Stone's whoops of relief.

Surprisingly, within fifteen minutes of their finding the trail they flew onto an asphalted road and then five minutes later they hit the highway to the city.

"Yeah!" Stone did not hide his exultation as they cruised toward their salvation. Indie swore silently that she would never let Stone drive her across the South African plains again. If there wasn't a driver to take her to the city, she wasn't going anywhere.

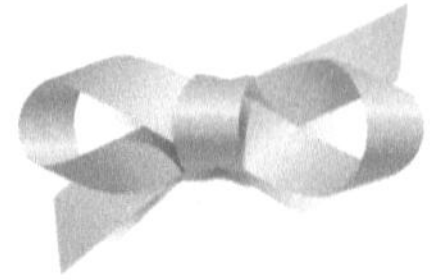

CHAPTER NINE

Stone was in love. He stood in the middle of his hotel room, as naked as the day he was born, and he was grinning from ear to ear.

Earlier this evening he'd seen his life flash before his eyes, the possibility of being devoured by wild animals a stark reality, and then, like a true warrior princess, Indiana Lane had come to the rescue.

He couldn't believe he was here celebrating being rescued by a woman. Hell, he should be ashamed of himself, getting lost like that. But in the end maybe it had been a good thing because it was that nerve-racking situation that had shown him what a rock Indie really was. He'd never met a woman like her in his life.

She'd shocked him with her calm composure in the face of probable death. And death by lion was not a pretty way to go. Instead of his having to calm a hysterical woman it was she who had kept a level head and kept him going.

To say he admired her was an understatement. And to say he loved her was the truth.

He'd felt it before tonight, of course. That first touch had been the start, and then that first kiss, and then that night when he'd almost gone a whole lot farther than just kissing. But tonight...

Tonight he'd seen a side of her that touched his core. She was honest, she was true and she was brave. And he wanted her in his life. But the big question was, would she have him? They'd known each other less than a month. If he told her how he felt would she really take him seriously? Questions, questions, questions. He shook his head. He would sleep on it and tomorrow he'd decide what to do. They planned to be up early next morning to visit Jenna and her new baby. And then he'd see what the day would hold.

. . ❧ . .

"ISN'T SHE ADORABLE?" Indie cooed as she held little Jessica Diamond Pringle in her arms. She shifted the baby to the crook of her arm and angled her so Stone could get a good look.

"She's beautiful," he said, and reached out to pat the tightly swaddled baby on its tiny pink hospital cap. He looked almost afraid to touch her. "And so tiny."

Jenna laughed as Kirk helped her sit up in the hospital bed. "The way she eats she won't be tiny for much longer. She gets that from her father."

"Hey." Kirk tried to sound hurt but the wide smile on his face spoiled it.

"Congratulations, Kirk." Stone reached out and shook his hand. "Great work."

"Great work?" Jenna looked indignant. "What part of the work did he do? I'm the one who looked like a cow for nine months and then had to be cut open. Sheesh!"

They all laughed at that and Indie leaned over to place Jessica in her mother's arm.

She and Stone had arrived at the hospital as soon as visiting hours began at ten o'clock and had been with the happy family almost two hours. She looked at Stone and caught his eye. He got the message.

"We're going to leave you now so mommy and baby can get some rest." He reached over and took Indie's hand. She almost pulled it away. What must Kirk and Jenna be thinking, seeing something like that? But when she looked at them they were so engrossed in the baby it seemed they hadn't noticed a thing.

Then she looked back at Stone. Boy, he was acting strange today. He'd been smiling a whole lot more than usual. Maybe he just loved babies. But then he'd captured her hand in his – in front of Jenna and Kirk – and when she tried to slip from his grasp he'd held on tight.

Could it be...no, it couldn't. There was no way. But – it was the weirdest thing – Stone was acting like a man in love.

She had no time to dwell on that, though, because he was pulling her toward the door.

"Bye, guys," Jenna called out. "Thanks for coming and thanks for the presents."

After the visit they had lunch in the exclusive Palais Royale Restaurant and then spent the afternoon together in the National Botanical Park. Then that evening as the sun was setting and they entered the hotel lobby Stone rested his hands on her shoulders and turned her toward him.

"Indie," he said, looking down at her with a half smile on his lips, "I had a wonderful day. I don't want it to end."

She looked up into his face and smiled back. "Me, too," she whispered.

"Will you have dinner with me tonight? There's...something I'd like to say to you."

Oh my God. Was the dream coming true? Indie had to fight to keep her face serene when what she really wanted to do just then was hop up and down in delight. "I would love to," she said, her voice calm, her smile just a little bit wider, but not too much.

She hadn't forgotten Tessa's lecture – you're a princess. Let him prove himself worthy of you. Act too eager and he'll take off running. Let him come to you.

"Great. Seven o'clock, then?"

"Let's make it seven-thirty," she replied. If she was guessing right tonight was going to be a special night and she needed to be ready.

"Seven-thirty it is."

Back in her hotel room Indie showered and slipped on the one dress she'd packed for the trip. It was a simple dress, but elegant – a 'little black dress' with a difference. Tessa had helped her pick this one out – spaghetti straps that showed off her shoulders, a V neckline that dipped deliciously low to show off just a hint of cleavage, a skirt that hugged her hips and tapered to her knees, and that one touch that never failed to draw male eyes to her legs – the slit at the side that went high enough to be alluring while maintaining that ever important air of decorum.

After accessorizing with a pearl necklace and matching earrings – on loan from Tessa – Indie sat down to do her makeup. Tonight was a night that called for makeup. She ran to her backpack and dug out her notebook. She flipped the pages till she found the one she was looking for – Tessa's instructions on how to do a killer makeup application. Indie decided to leave out the killer part, tone it down a bit. Right now all she wanted to know was how to make herself look pretty.

After much powdering and dabbing and penciling Indie sat back and surveyed herself in the mirror. Not quite the masterpiece Tessa had created but she could pass. The subtle shadow she'd applied on her lids and the eyeliner made the green in her eyes sparkle, and the peachy pink lipstick made her lips look soft and full. Ready for kissing. She giggled at the thought.

At exactly seven twenty-five she walked out of her room, purse in hand and high heels clicking as she headed for the elevator. And tonight she walked with confidence, not just because she'd practiced walking in high heels but because she knew – okay, maybe she didn't know but she had a really good feeling – that Stone was going to propose.

Then as the elevator doors opened the doubts came rushing back. Was he really going to propose or was that just wishful thinking on her part? She was just about to do the usual biting of her lip when she was in deep thought but she stopped herself just in time. Definitely not the thing to do when wearing lipstick. Then there was no time to ponder any further. The elevator doors opened and she stepped out, head high, and headed for the lobby.

Stone was already there, tall and impressive in a black dinner jacket and snow-white shirt open at the collar to reveal his strong tanned neck. As he approached he gave her a sexy smile. "Exquisite," he whispered and took her hand then leaned forward to give her a light kiss on the cheek.

So far so good. He was saying all the right things, making all the right moves. Now if he could only follow through right to the end she'd be a happy camper. And so would all the kids she planned to help with the fourteen million dollars.

As they walked out the front door a long black limousine pulled up in front and the uniformed chauffeur hopped out and opened the door for Indie. Stone got in behind and as soon as they'd made themselves comfortable, the car pulled away from the curb and merged into the traffic.

"Where are we going?" Indie asked.

"You'll see," Stone said, giving her a mysterious look.

She decided not to even think about what would come later. With a sigh she relaxed into the white leather seat and enjoyed the view of the city of Johannesburg at night.

It wasn't long before they pulled up in front of a building that made Indie's eyes widen and her jaw go slack. The place looked like a palace, like one of those castles in Versailles. But she hadn't died and gone to France, had she?

Stone leaned toward her. "Le Chateau de la Riviere," he said in a low voice. "They serve the best French cuisine in the country."

Indie nodded, still speechless, as she peered out the window at the majestic columns and the elegant statues that adorned the entrance. This was like no restaurant she'd ever seen before. Although it had lost its weight due to slang, the only word she could think of to describe it was 'awesome'.

Stone exited the limousine first then he held out his hand and helped her down. She felt like Cinderella being escorted by her prince.

He led her up the wide stone steps and into an immense marble-tiled lobby. They were immediately greeted by a black-uniformed host who seemed to have been expecting them.

"We have a private dining room." Stone explained as they were led down an adjacent hallway and then toward an elegant staircase. At the top they were ushered into an intimate room, ornately decorated with a statuette in the corner, elegant paintings on the walls and a rug with such an intricate design that it almost looked handmade. And in the middle of that rug stood a small round table set for two, a bouquet of white roses in the middle of it, and flower-shaped candles glowing softly around the vase.

Indie expelled her breath slowly, only then realizing she'd been holding it. "It's beautiful," she whispered.

"Glad you like it." Stone cupped her elbow and they walked over to the specially set table then as he helped her into her chair the host stepped forward. Stone quickly placed the orders and as soon as they were alone he reached over and took her hand in his. "I can't stop telling you how beautiful you look tonight."

Indie dropped her gaze, feeling the first flush of embarrassment. She wasn't used to receiving so much attention – and praise – from a man.

"You're one of the most beautiful women I've ever met," he said, "both inside and out." Then he gave a low, throaty laugh. "But I'm sure you hear that all the time."

No, not really, like...never. Indie said nothing. She just gave him a soft smile in response.

"As I told you, Indie, there's something I want to...have to say to you and I wanted to do this somewhere special." He looked down at their hands and then began to stroke her fingers with his thumb. "I was planning to wait until after dinner but...I can't keep this inside any longer. Indie, I..." He fell silent again.

Indie's heart lurched. Her palms grew damp and her breath caught in her throat. *Come on, say it. I can't breathe till you say the words.*

"I know you'll think this is crazy..."

No, I won't.

"...and you'll wonder how this is possible in such a short time..."

It's possible. It's possible.

"...but I've fallen in love with you, Indie."

He looked up at her then, deep into her eyes, and then he gave her hands a gentle squeeze. "I know this comes as a shock to you but I couldn't go another day without telling you how I feel."

He sighed and in his eyes was an earnestness that made Indie's heart soar. "What I'm saying is I want..." He looked down at their hands again and shook his head. "I can't believe I'm doing this to you."

Good heavens, man, just say the words. I'm running out of air. Indie could feel the smile on her face calcifying, she'd been holding that smile so long.

He drew in a deep breath. "Indie, I want-"

"To marry me?" she blurted. She just couldn't wait. She'd begun to grow faint from holding her breath that long.

He expelled his breath in a whoosh and on his face was a look of relief. "Yes. That's exactly what I was trying to say. I don't know why it wouldn't come out." He shook his head and gave a wry smile. "Probably because I was worried you'd think I'd gone round the bend."

Then his face turned serious. "So...what's your answer, Indie? I want you in my life. Always. Will you say yes?"

"Yes, yes, yes," she said, her eyes filling with tears. "Yes, Stone Hudson, I'll marry you. Tonight if you want. I love you, Stone, I really do."

"Sweetheart." The word was a soft whisper, then he lifted her hand to his lips and kissed it, almost with an air of reverence. Then he got up and pulled her up and into his arms and his kiss told her that the love he'd expressed was real. All his feelings and raw emotions were in that kiss.

When he finally released her Indie stared up at him, her heart brimming over with love. Then she whispered up at him, "When?"

He gave her a confused smile. "When?"

"Yes," she said as she stroked his arm. "How soon can we get married? I'm available now."

He laughed at that. "Well, I hadn't thought that far ahead but maybe we could make it a spring wedding. Or what about June? That's a popular time for weddings."

"That's too far away," she said with a little pout. "I can't wait that long to have you. What about now?"

He looked even more confused. "Now, as in tonight?"

She decided to back off a little so she wouldn't come off as crazy. "Well, maybe not tonight but my birthday is coming up soon and I thought...getting married to you on my birthday would be the best present I could ever have." Then she said cheekily, "Or maybe even the day before, just to be on the safe side."

He cocked an eyebrow. "The safe side?"

She shrugged. "Well, you know, in lots of cultures it's thought that the day begins at sundown of the previous day. I would love to get married as the sun sets on the eve of my birthday. That way I could wake up on my birthday as your wife."

He shook his head and gave her a loving smile. "You are something else, and that's why I love you so much. Who else would have thought of something so beautiful and so meaningful?"

She slid her arms around his waist and smiled up at him. "So we'll do it?"

"We'll do it," he said with a firm nod. "An eve-of- birthday wedding. Perfect." Then he bent his head to kiss her forehead. "And I hope you're not expecting any additional presents from me, young lady."

She laughed and swatted his arm. "Of course, I am. What do you take me for?"

He laughed, too. "Darling, I'll shower you with presents till you won't know what to do with them. It will be my greatest joy."

And then he bent his head and kissed her again, but this time it was no peck on the forehead. It was a real kiss, a passionate kiss that had her toes curling.

And as they kissed Indie thought life could not have been more perfect. Because more than anything, even more than the good she'd be able to do, she would be spending her life with the man of her heart. And she could hardly wait.

CHAPTER TEN

Life was hectic when you had a wedding to plan in just nine days. Indie and Stone had returned home after three days in Johannesburg and then she'd started planning. She was more than grateful that when she'd mentioned her best friend Stone had immediately offered to fly Tessa to South Africa to help her and to be her chief bridesmaid. She'd be arriving day after tomorrow, just seven days before the wedding.

The wedding would be held right there in the compound. Jenna and Kirk, Cook, and the staff at the boys' home, they'd all be there. And, of course, the boys. Everyone would share in the celebration. Stone's parents, his brother and sister and their families, and a few of his closest friends would be flying into Johannesburg and then would be coming to the compound on the morning of the wedding. The minister would drive in from a nearby township and Cook had identified a catering company who would supply all the food and drinks they'd need. It would take a lot of coordinating. Indie couldn't wait for Tessa to arrive. This sort of thing was her cup of tea.

Finally the day dawned when Tessa would come. Indie knew what time the flight was scheduled to arrive and she estimated how long it would take her friend to check through and then be transported out to the compound. She kept running to the cottage door to check if she saw the Jeep in the distance. At last, a distant cloud of dust appeared and then she heard the truck as it got closer and closer to the compound.

When Tessa finally arrived and hopped out the friends hugged and kissed and laughed at being together again.

"I missed you a lot," Tessa said, stepping back to look Indie up and down. "And you've changed since I saw you. You're glowing."

"I feel like I'm glowing," Indie said with a grin. "I've never been so happy in my life."

Tessa smiled at her and there were tears in her eyes. "I'm happy for you, Indie. So happy."

Indie got Tessa settled in her cottage then she took her for a tour of the compound. Then she looked at her watch. "Stone should be back by now. He'd gone with some of the men to check out a new pipeline they were running. Come on, let's go over to his place."

Stone was indeed there. He received Tessa warmly and even complimented her on her choice of friends.

Indie leaned over to Tessa. "He's biased," she said in a staged whisper that drew a laugh from both Stone and Tessa.

And as Indie laughed with them she could only give thanks that with her were the two people she loved most in the world. She was blessed.

· · ∽✿∾ · ·

STONE DECIDED HE HATED weddings. It wasn't that he didn't want to get married. That went without saying. He wanted Indie as his wife. There was no question about that.

What he hated was all this planning and organizing and rushing around. He liked order in his life. Regular, boring days, not this running around like a chicken without a head. Indie was forever giving him tasks, things to do with the wedding, and as much as he loved her he couldn't help wishing it was all over and done with. She and Tessa were excited, having endless meetings with decorators, but he wasn't cut out for this sort of thing. Now he was heading over to Indie's cottage to get an explanation on the note she'd left him. This was the day before the wedding and he wanted all his tasks over and done with so that he could relax. Unlike the fairer sex which seemed to thrive on turmoil, he was looking forward to a day of rest and recuperation before all the celebrations began.

Stone was surprised when he got to Indie's cottage and found the door wide open. He frowned but then he shrugged. They'd probably gone out onto the back porch for some fresh air. The days had gotten a bit muggy lately.

He stepped into the living room and, not surprisingly, there was no sign of them there. The back porch it was, then.

He was heading through the living room on his way to the back when he heard Tessa's high-pitched laugh and then Indie's lower-pitched one, and the sounds were coming from the bedroom. He smiled and changed direction, heading there instead. Women and their girl talk, he could bet.

He opened his mouth and was just about to call out to Indie when her words stopped him in his tracks.

"I'm finally going to get the money. Can you believe it, Tessa? Who would have known that l'il ole me could have gotten a man to propose in less than a month? With all that money I can do whatever I want. Isn't it great?"

What the hell? Stone felt like a wrecking ball had just slammed into his gut. Gotten him to propose? All that money? If they cut him right then no blood would flow. Everything inside him had turned to ice.

Indiana Lane, the woman to whom he'd declared his love, had seduced him so she could marry him for his money.

Stone's shock turned to hurt. And then it turned to a rage that crept up his entire body. He clenched his teeth and his nostrils flared. He'd gone down that road with a woman before, but never again. He would throw Indie out on her rear before he let her use him like that.

He marched over to the bedroom where the door stood slightly ajar. He pushed it open and stood in the doorway.

The women jumped and turned toward him. "Stone," Indie said, her eyes wide and her voice breathless, "when did you get here?"

"I just got here," he said through clenched teeth, "just in time to hear you planning how you're going to spend all my money."

"What?" Indie had been lying across the bed but now she raised up and stared at him. "What are you talking about?"

Stone laughed but the sound was bitter, even to his own ears. "Acting is definitely one of your strongest talents. Over there, acting so innocent. You deliberately seduced me, Indie, wormed your way into my heart, 'got' me to propose to you. Well, here's a little birthday present from me." He chuckled, warming to the idea of hurting her as much as she'd hurt him. "The wedding is off. I will not marry a woman who's only after my money. Damn." He slapped his palm against the door jamb. "And to think I saw you as the one woman I could trust. Jesus."

He shook his head and turned abruptly, intent on getting as far away from Indiana Lane as he could.

"Stone. Wait! That wasn't what I meant." He heard a rustle behind him like she was scrambling off the bed but he didn't stop to find out. She wasn't going to get another chance to practice her acting skills on him.

"Stone, please!" she cried and then she was at his side, and she was grabbing his arm, and she was clinging to him. "Let me explain."

He shrugged her off and kept on walking, his only acknowledgement of her a growl over his shoulder. "I want you out of here by sundown. I'll tell the driver to be ready with the truck."

INDIE RAN TO THE COTTAGE door but Stone was already yards away, striding purposefully in the opposite direction. He did not slow his pace and he did not look back and all she could do was stare at him in horror.

What could she say to him to make him stop? Her heart rose and lodged in her throat. She couldn't even call out to him.

Feeling like someone had just pulled her heart from her chest, she whirled away from the door and ran back to the bedroom where Tessa sat frozen on the bed.

"He's gone, Tessa. I couldn't stop him." She put a trembling hand to her forehead. "How could he think those things about me? How could he think I would do something like that?"

"Easy," Tessa said. She got up and walked toward Indie and put a hand on her shoulder. "He just heard something that sounded really bad. You and I know what you were talking about but he doesn't."

"But what he heard...it was out of context."

"Exactly. And that's why you have to go to him and explain what you really meant."

Indie pulled away from her and walked over to the window. She'd been surprised to see Stone at the door then shocked to witness his rage but now she was angry. "Me? I don't think so. If he could think something like that about me then maybe I don't want him to marry me." She was so angry she wanted to punch something. She walked over and punched the pillow.

"Calm down, Indie," Tessa walked over and caught her friend's arm then pulled her to sit down on the bed. "I know you're upset but what you said about not wanting Stone to marry you, you don't mean that. That's just the shock and anger talking."

Indie's shoulders slumped. She drew in a shaky breath then let it out but still she said nothing. She couldn't. The lump in her throat had grown huge and if she tried to speak she was going to break down in tears. And Indie didn't do tears, not for Stone Hudson, not for anybody.

"You have to go to him, Indie." Tessa reached out and put an arm around her shoulder. "Don't allow pride to make you lose out on this. You love Stone and I know he loves you, too."

Indie looked at her friend askance. What did she know? For someone who loved her he'd been pretty quick to walk away.

"I know he does, Indie," Tessa continued. "From the first time I saw the two of you together I could tell. He couldn't take his eyes off you. That man adores you."

Indie bit her lip. Maybe Tessa had a point. She didn't want to lose Stone, not like this. She had to give it a shot.

She looked over at her friend. "You're right. I have to talk to him about this." Then she gave a sad smile. "But after all that he still might not want me. We'd better have a plan B."

She got up off the bed and walked to the door. Then she turned and looked at Tessa. "I'll go find him. But just in case he still wants me out of here, start packing until I get back."

. . ◦§◦ . .

THE WORDS SWIRLED AROUND in Stone's mind. Every swear word in the book. How could he have been so stupid? He'd actually thought he'd fallen in love when all he'd been was seduced by a green-eyed witch who turned his insides to mush.

Love? He would never believe in that crap again.

He threw open the closet and began to rip his clothes down from the hangers. He dragged a duffel bag from behind the shirts and threw it onto the bed. There was no way he was going to stay here tonight. He'd told Indie he'd arrange for a ride for her but he would book a driver for himself, too. Even after she was gone this place would remind him too much of her.

Then he paused and stared ahead with glazed eyes. Now he'd have to do the dirty work. He had his parents to call, his brother and sister, his friends. Flights would have to be cancelled, caterers told not to come, the minister to explain things to. Jesus, what a mess!

He was muttering to himself as he turned back toward the bed with his clothes strewn all over it when he looked up and there in the doorway stood Indie.

Stone straightened and stared at her. "What are you doing here?" he asked, his voice cold.

She took a step forward then stopped. "Can we talk?"

He almost laughed at that. "We have nothing to talk about."

"You need to hear what I have to say."

"Why? I owe you nothing." He glared at her then shoved his hands into his pockets and looked away. He couldn't bear looking at her. She'd trampled his heart into the dust even though she knew he loved her. And, God help him, he still did.

"You hurt me, Indie," he said, his voice a low rasp. "Real bad. How can I ever trust you again?"

"Just hear me out, Stone. Please."

When he looked over at her she was staring at him with huge eyes, sad eyes. Despite his resolve his heart reached out to her. But still, he said nothing.

She drew in a breath then continued. "What you heard was totally out of context. I can't blame you for what you thought. I can't even blame you for being angry. But it's not what you think."

"Oh?" This was going to be good. What story was she going to cook up now?

"No, it's not."

Her voice was bolder now. She was probably thinking she could use her acting skills on him, worm her way back into his good graces. Well, it wasn't going to happen.

"I'm going to tell you the whole story and if you want to be angry afterward, then fine. But you deserve to know the truth."

"I appreciate that," he said, and he did not hold the sarcasm from his voice.

"The money I was talking about wasn't yours. It was left to me by my uncle."

He frowned. "Come again?"

She sighed. "I think I'd better start at the beginning." She glanced over at the armchair in the corner. "Do you mind?"

He shrugged. "Be my guest. I'm looking forward to hearing your story." He placed deliberate emphasis on the last word.

She walked over to the chair and sank into it with a sigh. Then she spoke. "On September twenty-three, exactly a month before my birthday, I was told by my late uncle's attorney that he'd left me fourteen million dollars. That's the money I was talking about."

"Fourteen mil-" Stone glared at her. "What do you take me for? A fool?"

"No, it's true. I can give you Mr. Marshall's number and you can call him yourself." She sat stiffly in the chair as she stared up at him.

"So what does that have to do with me marrying you?" Stone demanded, still not believing a word of what she was saying. "You said something about me proposing to you in a month."

Indie sighed. "That's the part...I'm not so proud of." She looked down at her hands then she looked back at him, her face resolute. "There was a condition to my getting the fourteen million dollars. I had to get married by my thirtieth birthday in order to get the money."

Stone almost laughed. "That's crazy."

"I know, but that's what the will says. My uncle wanted to make sure I didn't carry through on my threat never to get married or have kids. He wanted to maintain the bloodline and I'm the only hope."

"So you seduced me into marriage."

"No," she said quickly then, "well, yes. Sort of. It started out that way, where I was trying to get you to like me because...I already liked you."

Stone frowned. "You didn't even know me."

"I know," she said, confusion reflected on her face, "but that's the weirdest thing. From the first day we met I felt this...pull...and I knew if I were to ever get married you were the one I'd want to be with." She must have seen the disbelief on his face because she continued, "I could have married anyone, Stone. I could have picked a man from the street and married him. But...I wanted to fall in love. And I wanted the man I married...to love me, too."

"Love?" he scoffed. "You did this all for love? What about the money?"

"I wanted the money, too-"

"I thought so."

"I admit it. I did. But I wasn't planning on spending any of it on me."

"Yeah, right."

"No, really. Ask Mr. Marshall. In my file are the plans I submitted to him on how the money should be disbursed. All of it will go toward helping children in the countries where I've worked. I'd love..." she hesitated then gave him a shy look, "I'd love to be able to set up a children's home like the one you have here."

For a long while Stone stared down at her then he shook his head. "Your story, it's so crazy. Is any of it true?"

"All of it," she said, her voice firm. "The lawyer can verify everything."

He shook his head again. "Then, Indiana Lane, you are one heck of a woman." He walked over to where she sat in the chair. "Only you could have pulled it all off."

She stared up at him then she shook her head. "I haven't pulled off anything. I'm not married yet."

"No, but you will be. Tomorrow evening, if you'll still have me." He leaned down and pulled her up off the chair and into his arms. "I'm sorry I ever doubted you, Indie. Will you still marry me?"

She slid her arms around his waist and rested her head on his chest. "I don't know," she said. "I'm sure I could find an available man somewhere around here."

He chuckled and pulled her close. "I don't mind," he whispered then kissed the top of her head. "As long as it's me."

. . ❧ . .

NEXT EVENING, AS THE setting sun threw red, orange and yellow streamers across the sky, in the company of family, friends, co-workers and children, Stone Hudson and Indiana Lane exchanged wedding vows.

And as they danced together on the carpet of green grass to the sound of African drums, Indie went on tiptoe and tilted her mouth to whisper in her husband's ear, "I still want my birthday presents tomorrow."

And Stone's laughter, rich and deep and strong, echoed across the open plain.

EPILOGUE

"Congratulations, little Mommy. You have a beautiful baby girl."

Indie's eyes filled with tears as the nurse laid the baby on her breast. A baby of her very own. Who would have thought? And a loving husband by her side. Could anything be better than this? She smiled down at the little pink-cheeked baby on her breast then she looked across at Stone who was busy videotaping everything.

"Now take it easy," the nurse was saying. "Remember, you just had a C-section. Slow movements for today, okay?"

"Okay," she said obediently then turned to look up at the camera. "Put that camera down and come meet your daughter."

He did. Stone kissed Indie on the forehead then took the swaddled baby into his arms and this time he was more confident as he held the infant, more sure. Maybe it was because he was now a daddy. A real one.

"Now, in addition to your boys, you have a little girl of your own," she whispered to him. "When we leave Canada to go back to visit they're going to spoil her. You know that, right?"

"I know," he said, not taking his eyes from his daughter's face, "and I don't mind at all. My little Zuri Sky Hudson. She'll be able to handle them. She'll be tough just like her mommy. My little warrior princess."

Indie sank back into the pillows and smiled. She was already thinking of her next major project: how to keep Stone from spoiling their brand new daughter. That was going to be a tough one.

Thank you for reading!

<u>Free book offer:</u> Get your free copy of 'Rome for the Holidays' by joining my mailing list. On signing up you will be provided with the link to the story. Just visit my blog to join:

<u>http://www.judyangelo.blogspot.com/</u>
www.judyangelo.blogspot.com

• • ❧ • •

IF YOU'VE ALREADY READ this story and would simply like notification when I have new books out, still visit my blog and click on the sign-up link to join my mailing list. You may then choose to ignore the link to the free book. When new stories are out I'll keep you posted.

<u>http://www.judyangelo.blogspot.com/</u>

• • ❧ • •

My blog is also a great place to get more information
(Author profile, story summaries, announcements, etc.)
Come on by!

• • ❧ • •

If you wish to drop me a line, please send your e-mail to:
<u>judyangeloauthor@gmail.com</u>
judyangeloauthor@gmail.com.

• • ❧ • •

I would love to hear from you!

Sneak Preview of the next in the series:
BAD BOY BILLIONAIRES SERIES
VOLUME 9
Bedding Her Billionaire Boss

CHAPTER ONE

"With a name like Rockford St. Stephens, I can just imagine what he's like. Probably a pompous ass." Dana twisted a lock of hair around her left index finger as she stared out the window of her ex-boss's office.

Normally, she would have been impressed with the view of the city of New York from her position on the thirty-fifth floor of the building which housed Premier Holdings, but today she was seething. As she held the cordless phone to her ear she was glaring at the pedestrians way down below as they hurried along the streets of Manhattan.

"I mean, what kind of beast would bully a sixty-year-old man into selling out his business just like that? Mr. French was nowhere near retirement. That St. Stephen's guy forced his hand, Becky. I just know it."

"Now come on, Dana," her friend soothed. "Don't jump to conclusions. Remember, you're going to have to work with this man so it makes no sense to build up all this resentment against him."

"I don't have to work with him. I can quit." Dana's frown turned to a scowl. The very first time her new boss did anything to piss her off she would walk. Let him just try it.

"Yeah, and how easy do you think it's going to be to pick up another good paying job like this one?" Becky clucked in her usual 'mother hen' way. No matter that at twenty-five she was a year younger than Dana, she was always giving advice. The sad thing was, she was usually right. "In this economic climate you'd better hold on to what you've got. I could understand that attitude if you had another job lined up but you don't. Do you?" Becky's tone was firm. It was almost a reprimand.

Dana sighed. "You know I don't. That's just the impulsive me talking. As usual."

"Just think before you act, Dana. That's all I ask. And don't make assumptions." Becky chuckled. "And for heaven's sake, give your new boss a chance. For all you know he may be a sweetheart. Next time you call, it could be to tell me that he's a dreamboat and you're in love."

"I doubt it," Dana said drily. "Whatever this Rockford St. Stephens guy is like, I know I'll hate him."

"I appreciate the warm welcome."

Startled, Dana jumped and dropped the cordless phone. She whirled around to face the office door. There, big and bold and very imposing, stood a man who took her breath away.

She gasped and her hand flew to her mouth. Holy crapola! What had he heard? Everything? Just the end? But it didn't matter. The last comment she'd made had been the worst and she knew that her job with Premier Holdings was now history. Hell. Talk about bad timing.

Slowly, she slid her hand from her mouth and dropped her arms to her sides. Lifting her head, she stared him full in the face. Okay, so she'd misspoken. Put her foot in it, as Becky would say later when she told her she'd been fired. But she would not show fear. That was what her army officer dad had taught her and she would not let him down.

"Dana Daniels, I presume?"

The man walked into the executive office, his bold presence filling the spacious room, and stepped past her to drop his briefcase onto the huge mahogany desk that stood bare, all traces of Richard French now gone.

"Yes." That was all she said as her eyes ran up the length of him, from his shiny black shoes and up the obviously expensive business suit that covered a solid body and to his face, so cold and stern.

Dana swallowed. She almost dropped her gaze, his look was so intimidating. But no, she would be just as bold. It took everything in her but she faced his glare head on.

The unexpected visitor folded his arms across his chest as he looked down at her from what must have been at least six feet plus an additional two or three inches. As tall as she was, five feet seven inches in heels, he towered over her. "My executive assistant," he said, his voice surprisingly soft.

But Dana was not fooled. Soft and gentle, he was not. She could see it in his rigid stance and in the cynical twist of his lips. This man could be cruel...and she'd gone and pissed him off.

"Since you've already decided we'll start off as enemies, we might as well forgo the pleasantries and get down to business." He released his arms and walked around the desk where he pulled out the chair. "Go get your notebook or whatever it is you scribble in. You're going to organize a staff meeting for me tomorrow at ten o'clock. I have a quick phone call to make. Be back here in five minutes."

He sat down and reached for the phone then glanced over at her when she still stood there as if turned to stone. "Still here?" he asked, and this time there was no sardonic smile, only a scowl.

Dana blinked. He hadn't fired her. He expected her to come back and take notes. She'd been so shocked she hadn't even known how to react. But now, with his amber-colored eyes flashing in annoyance, she suddenly found herself with a great incentive to move. She had to get out of this line of fire.

Without another word she spun on her heels and marched through the door then reached behind her to close it with a firm click. Luckily no-one was in the outer office so there was no need to keep up appearances. Expelling her breath, she sagged against the solid oak door. What a way to start the morning.

Dana pushed away from the door and, knees trembling, walked toward her desk which was right outside the big boss's office. Now, instead of the kindly man with gray streaks in his hair, the one she had grown so used to seeing every day, she had found herself executive assistant to a cold, hard man who seemed as unyielding as the rock he'd been named after. Not a good situation...at all.

Throwing a quick glance at the door she made a dive for her cell phone and dialed Becky's number. She must have been waiting for the call because she picked up on the first ring. Dana didn't even bother with a greeting.

"You won't believe what just happened," she half gasped, half whispered into the phone.

"Your new boss walked in on you talking about him?" Becky asked drily.

Another gasp from Dana. "How did you know?"

"I heard him loud and clear, thanking you for the welcome. Then you dropped the phone." There wasn't an ounce of sympathy in Becky's voice. Some friend she was being right now.

But Dana had more news so she wouldn't tackle Becky on that just yet. "Yeah," she said, "but that's not the biggest surprise. The big shocker is, he didn't fire me."

"Even after hearing what you said?"

"Even after hearing that," Dana confirmed. "In fact, he told me he wants me back in his office in five minutes. Speaking of which, I've got to run."

"Wait," Becky yelled as she was about to hang up. "What does he look like? Dreamboat material?"

Dana paused then knitted her brow. "I don't know," she said, dragging the words as she thought about the question. "He's very handsome, that's for sure. Tall, with dark-blond hair and a pair of really intense gold eyes that bore into you like infrared beams. But dreamboat? I don't think so. Too cold and rigid. To qualify for 'dreamboat' status he should at least be approachable, don't you think?"

"Good point," Becky began and then the phone on Dana's desk began to ring.

"Miss Daniels," Rockford St. Stephens said when she picked up, "it's one minute past your deadline. Could you get in here, please?"

"Yes, Mr. St. Stephens." Her voice so cool it was frosty, Dana responded with a calm she didn't feel. She'd gotten off to a bad start with the new owner and she had a sinking feeling it was going to get worse. Before she'd even met the man she'd decided to hate him and then, before she'd had the chance to do that, she'd gone and given him a wonderful reason to hate her.

And now she'd be reporting to him five days out of every week. Great. Even though she hadn't been fired, now was probably a good time to start looking around for another job...just in case.

As soon as she'd hung up the phone she whispered, "See what I mean, Becky? A real beast. Anyway, got to go."

She grabbed her notepad and a pen then hopped out of the chair. At the door to St. Stephens's office she paused, straightened her pencil-slim skirt, and composed herself. Then she rapped sharply at the door and pushed it open.

She'd expected to find her boss sitting behind his desk, face in a frown, tapping his fingers on the hard wooden surface as he waited for her to show up. What she hadn't expected was to find him over by the credenza, his back to her, a chart spread out before him. From the door she could see that it was an organization chart and she knew what that meant. Staff cuts.

She shouldn't have been surprised. This was now the usual order – with take-overs or mergers the new management often chose to bring in workers from their old team or go for fresh blood. New perspective and all that. But, sensible though it might be, it hurt just the same. The thought that people might lose their jobs – herself possibly included – was depressing, to say the least.

St. Stephens looked up. "Finally," he said and there was no smile to accompany the word. "Have a seat. We have a lot to do today and I want to get started right away."

"Thank you, Mr. St. Stephens," Dana said demurely and went to sit in the chair in front of the big desk.

"Call me Rock. No need for formalities." He walked back to his desk and sat down then leaned back and tented his fingers. "I need to call a staff meeting first thing tomorrow and I need your help. Based on your reaction to having a new boss I can just guess the thoughts of the other members of staff." He shrugged. "And how can I blame them? All of this is unorthodox – the sudden departure of your boss, not much notice of the changes, a new man in the head office. So," he said, leaning forward, "let's put the rumors to rest."

By the time he was done speaking, Dana had an agenda of eight items including a review of the company's financial standing and a briefing on Rock's plans for the future of the organization. There was also a question and answer segment where the employees could sound off on their concerns.

"I need you, Dana." Rock's voice was solemn. "You know the team here, each person's temperament and how they'll respond to these changes. I'll need your guidance as we go through this transition."

Dana raised her eyebrows. He needed her? The way he'd come off as big and bold and brash, she didn't think big Mr. CEO would need anybody.

She laid her pen down on the notepad in her lap and gave him a direct stare. "How can I help you," she asked, "when I don't even know why you're here?"

For a second he looked taken aback by her question but then he nodded. "You're right. If you're going to be of use to me I'll have to take you into my confidence." For the first time since they'd met he smiled, a real smile, one that smoothed the furrows in his brows, a smile that reached his eyes. "You are my executive assistant, after all, the closest person to me in this firm."

For some strange reason those words brought a blush to her cheeks. She dropped her eyes, feeling the warmth rise in her face. He'd said 'the closest person to him' but he'd meant that in a professional sense. She knew that quite well, so why was her body acting so stupid?

"I'll let you in on a little secret."

She lifted her gaze, glad for the change of subject, but she was also way past curious. "Yes?"

"Mr. French and I, we've known each other for almost twenty years. He's the father of a high school buddy of mine." He tightened his lips and his eyes took on a faraway look. "He wanted as few people as possible to know this and I guess you'll have to be one of the few." His eyes refocused and he let out a sigh. "He's in trouble. He just recently found out he's got prostate cancer."

Dana gasped. Her heart pitched forward and fell to the pit of her stomach. No. Not kind and gentle Mr. French who had been her mentor these past four years. As if to protect her heart, her fingers curled round her notepad and she pressed it to her chest.

"He doesn't know how much time he has," Rock continued, his voice solemn. "The doctors are optimistic but he doesn't want to take any chances. Whatever time he has left, whether it's going to be measured in months or years, he wants to take full advantage of it. He loves the company but now he wants to spend as much time as he can with his wife and children." He shook his head then smiled. "And he told me he's got seven grandkids to play ball with. Even without the company he'll have his hands full."

Dana nodded, and with her new understanding of the reasons for her boss's hasty departure her resentment toward Rock St. Stephens dissipated. The man had stepped in to help a friend, not to force him out. "But why didn't he tell us before he sold the company?" she asked. "We would have understood."

Rock shook his head. "He didn't want anyone to know. He hated the thought of being pitied."

"But we wouldn't have-"

"Maybe not, but a man's got his pride." Rock almost sounded impatient. "He wanted this to be presented as strictly a business transaction, so let's leave it at that." He looked at her pointedly. "And I trust that this information will remain between the two of us."

Dana frowned. What did he think she was? A tattletale? She didn't air her annoyance, though. Instead, she asked, "So what do we tell the staff? They're going to come to this meeting expecting answers."

"I know." Rock leaned forward and rested his folded arms on top of the desk. "Here's what we'll say..."

• • ❧ • •

NOT BAD. Rock was feeling more than satisfied as he closed his office door behind him and walked across the room toward the plate glass windows overlooking New York's Fifth Avenue. He'd met with the staff of thirty-eight employees – a much smaller group than he'd ever worked with before – and had given each of them a chance to say their piece. Some said a lot, some said very little, and there were a few who looked like they had no idea what to say.

No matter. He'd answered all the questions thrown at him and had given the team the reassurance they needed. Without giving away too much, he'd told them that Mr. French had opted to enjoy an early retirement with his wife and had asked him, an old family friend, to take over the reins and do right by his staff. They didn't have to know that his time with them was limited. He had other, much larger companies to run. But for now, he'd focus his energies here and leave his other businesses to his competent cadre of managers.

Because at this corporation, his newest acquisition, there were questions to be answered and a major mystery to solve.

The fact was, Richard had shared a serious concern with him. Someone was embezzling company funds. Despite record sales of luxury vacation packages the company had shown no increase in its cash balance over the previous year. Something fishy was going on. But without real evidence, Richard had been loath to start making reports to the police. And so he'd begun doing his own investigation, checking the company books at nights when everyone had gone home. And then had come the disaster that had rocked him back on his heels. Cancer.

Now it fell to Rock to figure out what was going on. That had been at the forefront of his mind when he'd met with the employees and he'd paid close attention to every one of them, from the vice president of sales, Dennis Laing, to his sales agents, and from the financial controller, Sean Johnson and his team, to the human resources manager, the marketing representatives and the receptionist. And, of course, his own executive assistant, Dana Daniels.

Although, where Dana was concerned, Richard seemed to have gotten it in his head that she was above suspicion, something about having recruited her right out of college and being a mentor to her.

Rock had no beef with that but that didn't mean he wasn't going to investigate her just as thoroughly as the rest of the staff, no matter how distracting she was.

And she was distracting, with unreadable eyes of an intriguing color, a cross between hazel and violet. Amethyst, maybe? If you could describe eyes like that. He liked the way she wore her hair, letting it fall in soft waves down her back, the tendrils framing the softness of her cheeks. But it was the pout of her lips, so determined and defiant, that got him. The set of her mouth spoke of an impudence that was nothing short of provocative. And despite the fact that he wasn't much of a movie buff and never followed the Hollywood crowd, he couldn't help but notice her resemblance to Angelina Jolie.

As he remembered their first meeting Rock could not help smiling to himself. Ready to get down to business, he'd declined the receptionist's offer to walk him to Richard's old office and there he'd seen her, back to him, and even though he could not see her face he could read her defiance in her rigid stance - her back straight and her shoulders square.

And then when he'd heard her defiant declaration he'd known immediately he was in for a rough ride. This woman would be no pushover. He could see...and hear...that.

But no matter how strong-willed she was, she would fall in line soon enough. She'd better. He was here on a mission – to rescue the company from the parasite that was sucking it dry. And he would let nothing, not even a beauty like Dana Daniels, stand in his way.

Because he would find the culprit. He had absolutely no doubt about that.

To read more about Dana and Rock, get your copy of 'Bedding Her Billionaire Boss' from your favorite online retailer.

BAD BOY BILLIONAIRES
Volume 1 – Tamed by the Billionaire
Volume 2 – Maid in the USA
Volume 3 - Billionaire's Island Bride
Volume 4 - Dangerous Deception
Volume 5 - To Tame a Tycoon
Volume 6 - Sweet Seduction
Volume 7 - Daddy by December
Volume 8 - To Catch a Man (in 30 Days or Less)
Volume 9 – Bedding Her Billionaire Boss
Volume 10 - Her Indecent Proposal
Volume 11 - So Much Trouble When She Walked In
Volume 12 – Married by Midnight

· · ⚜ · ·

THE BILLIONAIRE BROTHERS KENT
Book 1 - The Billionaire Next Door
Book 2 - Babies for the Billionaire
Book 3 - Billionaire's Blackmail Bride
Book 4 - Bossing the Billionaire

· · ⚜ · ·

COLLECTIONS
BAD BOY BILLIONAIRES, Coll. I - Vols. 1 - 4
BAD BOY BILLIONAIRES, Coll. II - Vols. 5 - 8
BAD BOY BILLIONAIRES, Coll. III - Vols. 9 - 12
THE BILLIONAIRE BROS. KENT - Books 1 - 4
BAD BOY BILLIONAIRES, Double Coll. - Vols. 1 - 8
BAD BOY BILLIONAIRES, Mega Coll. - Vols. 1 - 12

. . ✢ . .

HOLIDAY EDITIONS
Rome for the Holidays - Novella
Rome for Always - Full-length Novel

. . ✢ . .

The NAUGHTY AND NICE Series
Volume 1 - Naughty by Nature

. . ✢ . .

COMING SOON
THE CASTILLOS
Book 1 - Beauty and the Beastly Billionaire

. . ⚜ . .

Author contact:
judyangeloauthor@gmail.com

. . ⚜ . .

Connect with me on Facebook:
Judy Angelo - Facebook[1]

. . ⚜ . .

Cover Artist: Ramona Lockwood (Covers by Ramona)

---

1. https://www.facebook.com/pages/Judy-Angelo-Author/207657399403357?ref=hl

Don't miss out!

Visit the website below and you can sign up to receive emails whenever JUDY ANGELO publishes a new book. There's no charge and no obligation.

https://books2read.com/r/B-A-WPD-PFN

Connecting independent readers to independent writers.

Did you love *To Catch a Man (in 30 Days or Less)*? Then you should read *Her Indecent Proposal*[2] by JUDY ANGELO!

Book 10 of 12 -

GIVE ME A BABY...NO STRINGS ATTACHED

Melanie Parker is at the top of her game. Thirty-three years old, owner and CEO of Parker Broadcasting Corporation, with assets totaling over a billion dollars. There are many who would die to be in her shoes. But there's one thing Melanie feels is missing from her life. A child. She's always dreamed of one day being a mother but just never found the time to fall in love. And now time is running out. So she seeks out the one man who she knows can give her

2. https://books2read.com/u/mdNPEb

3. https://books2read.com/u/mdNPEb

what she wants and will demand nothing in return, a man who's a billionaire himself.

Sloane Quest can't believe it when the owner of Parker Broadcasting Corporation – his biggest competitor in the media business – makes him the craziest of all proposals. The decision he makes is quick, and it probably defies all reason, but he has an ulterior motive which will not be denied.

Complications, intrigue and a baby bargain in the middle. Can love conquer all?

Read more at judyangelo.blogspot.com.

Also by JUDY ANGELO

Bad Boy Billionaires - Where Are They Now?
Tamed by the Billionaire - The Sequel

Billionaire Bachelorettes of Bel-Air
In Bed with the Enemy

Billionaire Brotherhood
The Billionaire Brotherhood III, Vols. 9 - 12

Historias Multimillionarias para Navidad
Rome para Navidad

MADE FOR THE MOVIES Fantasy Romance
Trading Spaces

Back from the Future
Back from the Future with BONUS Trading Spaces

Multimillonarios Machos
Domada por el Multimillionario
Domado por el Multimillionario, Bilingual Version

NUGGETS OF KNOWLEDGE
How to Write a Romance Novel

The BAD BOY BILLIONAIRES Series
Sweet Seduction
Daddy by December
To Catch a Man (in 30 Days or Less)
Bedding Her Billionaire Boss
Her Indecent Proposal
So Much Trouble When She Walked In
Married by Midnight
Bad Boy Billionaires - Collection II, Vols. 5 - 8
Bad Boy Billionaires Mega-Collection Vols 1 - 12

THE BILLIONAIRE BROTHERHOOD
Tamed by the Billionaire (Roman's Story)
Maid in the USA (Pierce's Story)

Billionaire's Captive Island Bride (Dare's Story)
Dangerous Deception (Storm's Story)
To Tame a Tycoon
The Billionaire Brotherhood Coll. III Bks 9 - 12
The Billionaire Brotherhood Collection I, Vols. 1 - 4
The Billionaire Brotherhood Books 1 - 8

The Billionaire Brothers Kent
The Billionaire Next Door
Babies for the Billionaire
Billionaire's Blackmail Bride
Bossing the Billionaire
The Billionaire Brothers Kent

The BILLIONAIRE HOLIDAY Series
Rome for the Holidays
Rome for Always
Home for the Holidays

The Castillos
Beauty and the Beastly Billionaire
Training the Tycoon
The Mogul's Maiden Mistress
Eva and the Extreme Executive
The Castillos - The Collection

The Comedy, Conflict and Romance Series
Taming the Fury
Outwitting the Wolf
Romancing Malone
Comedy, Confict & Romance - The Collection

The Naughty and Nice Series
Naughty by Nature

Standalone
The Billionaire's Bold Bet

Watch for more at judyangelo.blogspot.com.

About the Author

New York Times & USA Today best-selling author, Judy Angelo, considers herself a 'traveling writer'. She currently resides in Ontario, Canada but prior to that she called New York and then Illinois home. She has also spent considerable time in the Caribbean, Latin America and Europe. She loves to travel as it provides her with interesting and diverse settings for her stories.

Judy fell in love with romance novels as a teenager and has never lost her passion for these stories of love and life, conflict and reconciliation, relationships and family. For her, it was a natural progression from reading romance novels to writing them. So far, she has written over 70 romance novels, including the best-selling Bad Boy Billionaires series. Her other series include The Billionaire Brothers Kent, The Castillos, and the Comedy, Conflict & Romance series.

She hopes to continue entertaining her readers with intriguing stories for many years to come.

Website - www.judyangelo.blogspot.com

I would love to hear from you! judyangeloauthor@gmail.com

Read more at judyangelo.blogspot.com.